MW00445838

# WAYNE STINNETT

# FALLEN TIDE

## A JESSE MCDERMITT NOVEL

✦ ✦ ✦ ✦

*Caribbean Adventure Series*
*Volume 8*

DOWN ISLAND PRESS

2015

Published by DOWN ISLAND PRESS, 2014
Travelers Rest, SC

Copyright © 2015 by Wayne Stinnett
All rights reserved. No part of this book may be reproduced, scanned, or distributed in any printed or electronic form without express written permission. Please do not participate in or encourage piracy of copyrighted materials in violation of the author's rights. Purchase only authorized editions.

Library of Congress cataloging-in-publication Data
Stinnett, Wayne
Fallen Tide/Wayne Stinnett
p. cm. - (A Jesse McDermitt novel)
ISBN-13: 978-0692575055 (Down Island Press)
ISBN-10: 0692575057

Graphics by Tim Ebaugh Photography and Design
Edited by Clio Editing Services
Proofreading by Donna Rich
Interior Design by Write.Dream.Repeat. Book Design

This is a work of fiction. Names, characters, and incidents are either the product of the author's imagination or are used fictitiously. Any resemblance to actual persons, living or dead, businesses, companies, events, or locales is entirely coincidental. Most of the locations herein are also fictional, or are used fictitiously. However, I take great pains to depict the location and description of the many well-known islands, locales, beaches, reefs, bars, and restaurants throughout the Caribbean, to the best of my ability.

# FOREWORD

A lot of work by a lot of people went into this book. Many ideas for plot and characters came from my usual sources. My wife, Greta, heads that list as always. I couldn't imagine doing this without her support and guidance.

The underlying plot for *Fallen Tide* from the very inception of this book was the reunion at the end. The idea for that came from one of my readers, Cliff Barth, who lives in Tehachapi, California. Thanks, Cliff.

Another reader provided so much help in the little details of one character that I made him the character. Dave Parsons is a real-life retired Army CWO4 and Special Agent with the Army's Criminal Investigation Command. He currently splits his time between Massachusetts and California.

Fellow author Paul Deaver is an active-duty Army helicopter pilot. The idea for the Predator suit was his. Watch for Paul's first novel to be published very soon.

Thanks also to my beta reading team, Alan Fader, Marc Lowe, David Parsons, Jeanne Gelbert, Dana Vihlen, Ted Nulty, Debbie Kocol, Charles Hofbauer, Mike Ramsey, Joe Lipshetz, and Tom Crisp. These folks have a ton of specialized knowledge and experience pertaining to details in my books. Without them, the reading experience wouldn't be anywhere near as good or accurate. Your input has been extremely valuable in making this book better than it was.

# DEDICATION

*Dedicated to the men and women who make up America's first responders. From the Coast Guard and National Guard, to our local law enforcement and firefighters, these brave men and women in uniform will move toward the sound of chaos, when everyone else is moving away from it.*

"Bits and pieces have to come together. I'm like a blue tick hound, running back and forth at the edge of the swamp, nose in the air, wondering if there is a trail worth following. And kind of hating going into the mud, snakes and gators."

- **Travis McGee,** Freefall in Crimson, 1981

If you'd like to receive my twice a month newsletter for specials, book recommendations, and updates on coming books, please sign up on my website:

WWW.WAYNESTINNETT.COM

## THE CHARITY STYLES CARIBBEAN THRILLER SERIES
*Merciless Charity*
*Ruthless Charity* (Summer, 2016)
*Heartless Charity* (Winter, 2017)

## THE JESSE MCDERMITT
## CARIBBEAN ADVENTURE SERIES

*Fallen Out*
*Fallen Palm*
*Fallen Hunter*
*Fallen Pride*
*Fallen Mangrove*
*Fallen King*
*Fallen Honor*
*Fallen Tide*
*Fallen Angel*
*Fallen Hero* (Fall, 2016)

The Gaspar's Revenge Ship's Store is now open. There you can purchase all kinds of swag related to my books.
WWW.GASPARS-REVENGE.COM

# FALLEN
# TIDE

# MAPS

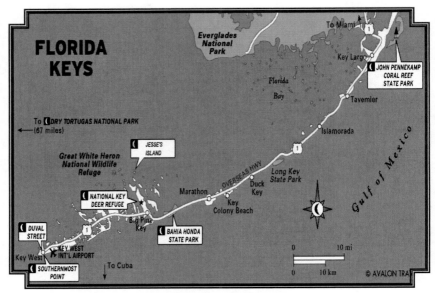

*The Florida Keys*

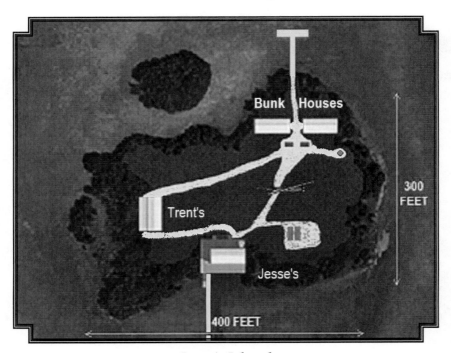

*Jesse's Island*

# CHAPTER ONE

I t was the large number of lobsters clustered together that caught my attention, distracting me from my
morning swim. Every morning, I swim the same three
miles, looking at the same bottom. I know the contours
of the sea floor and where to make my turn, without having to look up. But every morning it's different. Every
morning, there's something new to see. Which is why I
started wearing swimmers' goggles a few months back.
Lobsters are nocturnal, but occasionally during my swim
I'll see a late forager still out on the grass flats after sunrise. Sometimes I'll see a nurse shark as well, still hunting for late-foraging lobsters. Usually, both are tucked
away in the thousands of cracks, crevices, and ledges, or
the many patch reefs in the back country of the Middle
Keys where I live.

   The presence of so many lobsters, along with what
appeared to be an equal number of crabs of assorted spe-
cies and sizes, piqued my curiosity. I stopped to watch
as the occasional damselfish or blue-striped grunt dart-

ed into the fray. A thick dead branch of what looked like staghorn coral stuck out from the roiling group of crustaceans and fish. Normally, a broken piece of dead coral wouldn't get my attention. As I floated on the surface, I realized it wasn't a coral branch at all. I knew this because staghorn coral branches rarely wear a wristwatch.

Lifting my head to take a breath, I pulled off my goggles to determine my location. I was in about eight feet of water nearly a mile from my island on the edge of Harbor Channel, and there wasn't a boat anywhere in sight. Knowing it was slack tide didn't change what I knew I had to do. The tide would be rising very soon, meaning the severed limb would be carried away with the current. If a hungry shark didn't find it first.

Floating above the edge of the channel just a few yards away was one of Carl's and my lobster trap floats, the trap itself set in twenty feet of water against the steep drop-off. Though I hated to do it, I knew what had to be done.

Putting my goggles back on, I arched forward and dove. When I reached what I now knew to be a detached left arm and hand, the lobster and all but a handful of tenacious crabs scattered. I grabbed the arm at the denuded end, where the bone stuck out, and returned to the surface, the last couple of crabs dropping off as I rose. Dangling my grisly find, I sidestroked to the float and took a deep breath before submerging and pulling myself along the trap line, one-handed. The irony of that set in. I had a third hand, but was only using my own right.

It was only twenty feet to the bottom, but I had to pause several times to equalize the pressure in my ears, trying not to drop the arm or let go of the rope for long.

Reaching the trap, I quickly opened the top and tipped the concrete-based trap on its side, releasing a half dozen lobsters, before thrusting the arm inside and closing it again. At least the arm would still be here when I returned in my skiff, but it was a damned shame to let all those lobsters go.

Swimming quickly back to the north pier, I dried off as I hurried toward the foot of the pier. Spotting Carl working in the aquaculture garden, I called out to him as I jogged toward my house and the dock area beneath it.

Carl and his wife, Charlie, are the caretakers of my little island in the Content Keys, north of Big Pine Key. He'd been a shrimp boat captain until a couple years ago, when the two of them came to work for me and built a small house on the west side of the island. Carl still owns the shrimp boat, but no longer goes out, content to fish, dive, and work on projects around the island. His former first mate, who worked for me for a short while, now skippered the *Miss Charlie*.

"Carl, drop what you're doing and call the sheriff. Have them send a boat out to where the number four trap is located."

Carl looked up as I ran past. "Poacher?"

Trap poachers were common in the Keys, but rarely ventured this far north. My island is six miles from the nearest road, and nearly double that taking all the cuts and channels to get here.

"Not unless he's missing an arm," I shouted back. "Tell them to hail me on the VHF."

As I disappeared under the house, Carl headed up the steps to the deck, the only spot on the island where a cell phone can get a signal. While I untied and jumped

3

aboard my Maverick Mirage flats skiff, I heard him talking on the deck above my charter boat. Punching the button on the key fob, I activated the release on one of the large doors, and it slowly began to swing open on giant spring-loaded hinges.

The outboard started instantly, and I idled out from under my little house and into Harbor Channel, just a few yards to the south. Turning sharply into the channel, I brought the little boat up on plane and steered a rhumb line toward where I knew our trap was located. Approaching it, I stood up at the helm and looked all around. There wasn't another boat in sight and it'd been several days since we'd heard or seen one.

Coming off plane, I approached the trap's green-and-yellow float, then reversed the engine and came to a stop, drifting in the still water right next to it, and shut down the outboard. I quickly tossed the anchor in the direction of the spot where I'd first seen the arm and let out a good twenty feet of rode. It was still half an hour before the current would start picking up, the tide carrying nutrient-rich water from the Glades through the long archipelago known as the Florida Keys, and into the Atlantic, renourishing the reef that thrived there. I was pretty sure the sheriff's office would want to know exactly where I'd found the arm.

As I was pulling up the trap, a familiar voice came over the radio. "Deputy Phillips hailing *MV Gaspar's Revenge*."

After hoisting the trap and its grotesque contents aboard, I grabbed the mic. "I'm on the skiff, Marty. Go to sixty-nine."

Deputy Marty Phillips was dating my daughter Kim, who was in college up in Gainesville. Maintaining a long-distance relationship wasn't easy for them, but they seemed to be handling it well. She came down here once a month and he went up there just as often.

When I'd changed frequencies, Marty hailed me again. "Carl called something in and told dispatch to hail you. What's up, Jesse?"

"Do you have a diver with you? I found an arm."

There was a moment of silence. "Did you say you found an arm? You mean like a human arm?"

"Roger that," I said, opening the lid on the trap and examining it more closely. "Looks like a man's. Severed at the middle of the upper arm, and the bone's cut pretty clean."

"I'll have another boat with divers aboard on the way in a few minutes. Where are you exactly?"

"Northeast of my house about a mile," I replied. "On the north side of Harbor Channel, just across from Cutoe Banks. Tide's slack right now, but it'll change in less than an hour."

"I'm not far. I'll be there in ten minutes. Have you moved it?"

"Well, yeah," I replied. "I spotted it on the bottom during my morning swim and thought you guys might want to have a look at it before a hungry spinner came along and stole it from the crabs and lobster that were feasting on it. I stuck it in one of my traps and just hoisted it on deck. I'm anchored over the spot where I found it."

"That'll have to be good enough. See you in a few minutes."

"Roger that. Back to sixteen."

Switching the radio back to the hailing frequency, I sat down at the helm and studied the thing in the trap. What was left of the arm was nearly bare bone from where it was cut off to just below the elbow. The flesh on the forearm moved, giving me a start. Then a small spider crab wiggled free and fell between the two bones of the upper forearm, just below the elbow.

The rest of the arm was fairly intact, just a few scrapes and cuts, probably where it'd been dragged and rolled across the bottom with the current. Looking south, I could see in my mind's eye how the current flowed through the back country. We've had stuff wash up at low tide that obviously came from the Atlantic, floating more than ten miles through the several natural cuts and channels.

Looking back at my grotesque find, I noticed that the fingers were thick and meaty, the nails trimmed short. There was part of a tattoo left on the top part of the forearm, though it looked to be old and faded. The watch was cheap, but waterproof.

Marty arrived a few minutes later, cutting across the flats from Spanish Channel into Harbor Channel, his blue lights flashing. As it slowed, the big center console came down off plane and he idled up alongside. I tossed a couple of fenders over and helped him tie off.

"Divers will be here in twenty minutes or so," Marty said as he stepped over the gunwale and looked down into the lobster trap. Squatting, he looked at it more closely and then glanced up at me. "Where exactly did you find it?"

Looking at my anchor line and over the side at the bottom, I pointed off to the north. "Just a few yards beyond the edge of the drop-off."

Sitting back on the casting deck, Marty removed his sunglasses and dipped them in the water before pulling a handkerchief from his pocket and wiping the water off. "Sure looks like a clean cut on the end of the bone, but the coroner will be able to tell for sure. You make anything of the tattoo?"

"Some kind of tribal design, maybe. Black ink, faded to gray. I don't think it's military."

"Could be a gang tat," he offered. "But yeah, it looks to be older."

"What do we do now?" I asked.

"Wait for the divers and coroner, I guess. I just respond to calls and write tickets to people breaking the law."

Stepping back over to his boat, he lifted the seat in front of the console, took two water bottles out of the cooler, and handed me one.

"Thanks," I said, taking the bottle and drinking half its contents. "Any other body parts wash up lately?"

"Nothing that I've heard," Marty replied. "But, like I said, I'm not an investigator."

Minutes later, hearing the distant whine of an outboard, I stood up and looked to the east. "Looks like your divers."

Marty and I watched as another sheriff's boat pulled alongside, with a deputy and two divers aboard, already suited up. As one of the divers started to tie off to Marty's boat, I said, "Best if you drop your own tackle. We're on mine, and once the current picks up, it won't be big enough to hold all three boats in place."

I recognized the deputy at the wheel, but didn't know his name. I'd never seen the two divers before. "Did you find it in that trap?" the deputy asked.

"No, I found it a few yards that way," I replied, pointing in the direction of my anchor. "Idle around us and drop your hook near mine. That's pretty close to where I found it."

As the deputy maneuvered around us, another boat crossed the flats and headed toward us. It was a larger center console, with blue lights flashing. On board were another deputy in uniform and two more divers, still struggling into their equipment. Two more men, both dressed in gray coveralls, were with them. One was older than the others by several decades.

"That's Doc Fredric," Marty said. "He's the chief medical examiner, lives in Marathon."

"Seen him around," I replied.

Minutes later, after Marty scrambled and added his anchor close to where mine was, all four divers rolled backwards into the water to begin their search for the rest of the body.

"Mind if I step over?" the doctor asked.

I nodded by way of reply and moved toward him to give a hand. But the old man easily stepped down to my skiff by himself. His hair was snowy white and his skin was tan and weathered. Squatting down, he pulled on a pair of blue rubber gloves and examined the arm in the trap.

"Pass your back board over, Marty," Fredric said without looking up.

With the back board on the deck, Fredric lifted the limb from the trap and placed it on the board. It looked a lot more out of place there than in the trap. He then lifted the board up onto the casting deck and examined it from end to end.

"How long ago did you find it, Captain?"

"Less than an hour ago, Doctor. Just call me Jesse, everyone else does."

He looked up at me, over the top of his glasses. "Jesse McDermitt?"

"Yes, sir," I replied.

He fluttered a blue hand around. "Just Leo or Doc, Jesse." Then with a half smile he said, "I've heard of you. This isn't your handiwork, is it?"

The glint in his sharp blue eyes told me he was pulling my leg. "Might have been," I replied with a crooked grin. "Hard to keep track."

The older man laughed and then motioned me over. When I squatted beside him, he produced a small magnifying glass from his pocket and handed it to me. "Look close at the proximal end of the humerus."

Guessing that he meant the end where the bone was cut, I held the glass close to it and leaned in. The end of the bone was cut straight across and fairly smooth. "A saw of some kind?" I asked.

"Look just to the left of the end. See that notch?"

About a quarter of an inch down the bone, there was indeed a straight notch, probably a quarter of an inch wide and a fraction of that deep. It was on the side of the bone where the biceps would be, if that muscle were still there.

"What caused that?" I asked, returning the little magnifying glass.

"Chain saw, most likely," Doc replied, leaning in closer.

"A chain saw?" I asked. "I thought that only happened in movies or TV."

"Happens more than you'd think," the old man said. "There's a whole science on the many cutting tools used to dismember a body. The blade must have bounced off the bone with the first attempt."

Looking at the bone without the magnifying glass, the notch was barely visible, and he'd found it without the glass. "What else do you see, Doc?"

The old man grinned. "Everything, Jesse. I've seen everything." He bent over the end of the bone and looked again, handing me the magnifying glass. "Look here. See that small spur on the back side of the bone?"

I looked through the glass at the end of the bone, where it'd been cut. "Yeah, I didn't notice it before."

"You do much carpentry, Jesse?"

"Some. Why?"

"When you cut a two-by-four with a power saw, you sometimes leave a spur, almost always on the end that's supported, when the other end falls off."

"I thought you said chain saw, Doc?"

He looked at me with eyes twinkling the way a good teacher's would, when a pupil grasps a concept. "Yes, I did. The length of the spur is dependent on the amount of leverage applied to the blade. With a circular saw, the weight of the tool and the push of your hand puts most of the force on the severed end. If you use a lightweight handsaw, you rarely have a spur, or it's very small. With a power saw, or in this case, a chain saw, you're able to apply more leverage, snapping the board when the blade is still further from the end."

"A good argument for using hand tools," I said, handing the glass back once more. "But wouldn't the pressure exerted with a chain saw be directly on the cut?"

"You have a sharp mind," Doc said with a quick smile. "Once I get this back to the lab, I think I'll be able to confirm why the spur is where it is."

Turning to Marty, he said, "Call it in, son. Desecration of a corpse at the very least, but I'm guessing this happened during the commission of a homicide. White or Hispanic male, thirties or forties, not married, close to six feet tall and muscular. Blue-collar type, probably made his living on the water."

# CHAPTER TWO

The man's head slumped forward as his body sagged. Jerking back upright, he looked around the dark confines and wondered how long they'd been held. It'd probably been an hour since he'd awakened with a terrible throbbing in his head, but he couldn't be sure, as he kept nodding off. Darius Minnich was unaccustomed to such harsh treatment. He looked over at his wife of six years. Celia was even less accustomed.

Darius was twenty-five years older than his second wife. She'd been a research assistant with his company when they'd first met. CephaloTech was struggling and near bankruptcy then. His first wife had left him, filed for divorce, and taken nearly everything he had, leaving him destitute and almost penniless.

Two months after the divorce was final, came the company's big breakthrough in their fiber-optic suit technology. Her lawyer had been good, but had neglected to attach future earnings to the alimony payment, and Darius became a fifty-two-year-old multimillionaire overnight. His alimony payment now represented less than one percent of his income, and there was nothing she or her lawyer could do about it.

Celia had been a nubile twenty-seven-year-old lab assistant at the time. Tall, blonde, and shapely, with a quick mind and wit, she knew what she wanted in life, and suddenly her newly-single boss had it. Some women peak in their early twenties, but not Darius's trophy wife. At thirty-three, she was even more beautiful than the night she'd easily seduced him in the lab, after the big announcement of the DoD contract and the subsequent celebration. They were married two weeks after that. Darius had even sent his ex-wife an invitation to the wedding. It was held on the exclusive private island of Petit Saint Vincent, in the Lesser Antilles. She didn't come.

Celia was still passed out. Like Darius, her feet were tied to a post and her arms to a crossbeam at shoulder height. Her blouse was torn at the shoulder. She'd fought back against their attackers with a vengeance. The dried blood on the left shoulder of her light green blouse proved it. It had come from a gash in her forehead where one of their attackers had hit her with the butt of an assault rifle.

Darius calculated that they'd been trussed up like this for nearly a full day. However, with no windows in the dark and musty room they were in, he couldn't be certain. How long they'd been knocked out before getting here, he couldn't even guess at. His mouth was parched, his lips cracked and dry. Their captors had gassed them shortly after the attack, and the effect of the gas was only now dissipating. It could have been hours or days, he had no way of knowing.

Hearing a moan, he looked to his left and saw that Celia was just beginning to come around. He'd woken twice that he knew of since the attack, but Celia had already been beaten unconscious before they were gassed. He had no idea if she'd awakened before now.

"Celia," Darius whispered, though he didn't know why. "Are you okay?"

Slowly, she lifted her head, her normally lustrous blond hair now matted with blood and hanging down over her face. When she tried to shake her hair back, she winced in pain. "Yeah, I think so. Where are we?"

"I don't know. All I remember is someone putting something like an oxygen mask over both our faces right after one of them hit you."

Celia started to say something more, but just then a door opened just twenty feet in front of them. The brilliant glare from outside hurt both their eyes, and they tried to turn away as two men walked in, one carrying a large object in his right hand. The door slammed shut, the hollow ring echoing throughout the room.

"I see you are awake," one of the men said, with a slight accent Darius couldn't place.

He stopped a few feet in front of Darius. The other man stood off to his right, slightly behind the first man. Darius could no longer see anything, his eyes blinded by the sudden light. He tried to squint to see the man, when suddenly the beam from a flashlight blinded him again.

"You have something I need," the man said. "You will make arrangements for it to be delivered to me electronically."

Turning his head from side to side, trying to avoid the bright light, Darius finally lowered his head. "I have no idea what you want."

"Come now, Mister Minnich. You have no idea?" He crossed over to Celia and took a handful of hair in his hand and jerked her head up, causing her to scream in pain. "Go ahead and scream, whore!" the man yelled. "Scream all you want, nobody will hear you. Oleg, look at her. She is beautiful, no?"

"Keep your hands off my wife," Darius grunted.

"Or what, *pindos*?" the man snarled, ripping Celia's blouse open, scattering pearl buttons across the dirt floor. "I give the orders here." The man pulled aside the tattered blouse, exposing Celia's firm belly and frilly satin bra. "Oleg, how much do you think this whore will bring?"

"Half a million rubles, easy," the man holding the flashlight replied, with a grunt. "If it survives."

"What do you want from us?" Darius yelled.

The man released Celia's hair and her head slumped back down. He took the flashlight from Oleg and stepped over in front of Darius. Pulling his head up by the hair, the man shined the light in Darius's face. "Your individual stealth technology. All of it."

"No!" Darius replied. "I won't do it. I can't. You may as well just kill me."

"Oh, I am not going to kill you, Mister Minnich. However, you may wish yourself dead in the very near future." The man released Darius and stepped back. "Oleg? What do you think a one-armed whore will bring?"

Darius heard a sputtering sound, followed quickly by a loud roar. The man turned the flashlight toward

Oleg. Darius watched in horror as Oleg wielded a chain saw and revved the engine, filling the small confines of the room with acrid oil smoke. Oleg slowly approached Celia, raising the chain saw to shoulder level.

Somewhere in the back of Darius's mind, a memory exploded into clarity. Just after the mask had been placed over his face, he had seen this same man using the same chain saw to dismember one of Darius's crewmen on the yacht. The crewman was alive and awake when it happened.

"Stop!" Darius yelled, the pain and revulsion stinging his mind. "I'll tell you anything, give you anything you want! Just don't hurt my wife!"

# CHAPTER THREE

By midafternoon, I was sitting at my favorite watering hole, the *Rusty Anchor*, in Marathon. Being a Friday, I was there to catch up on the coconut telegraph and wait for my girlfriend, Linda. She works for FDLE, out of their Miami office, and always leaves work early on Friday to meet me here and spend the weekend on the island.

"I haven't heard of anyone missing, bro," Rusty said. "And if any watermen in the area were missing, I'd know about it."

It was true. If anything of significance happened in the Middle Keys, Rusty Thurman would know about it within hours. Half a day at most, for the rest of the island chain. I'd known Rusty all of my adult life. We'd served together in the Corps until he got out after his first tour. A short man, barely five and a half feet tall, he weighed a good three hundred pounds, but had recently started working to get some of the weight off. It never seemed to slow him down, though.

"Doc Fredric feels pretty certain he was a waterman," I said. "Maybe a crewman from a boat that was passing through?"

"How could he tell that from just an arm?" Rusty asked.

"Not only that, but he could tell his height and build and what kind of saw was used to cut the arm off," I replied.

"Could be a cruiser, man," Jimmy said. "Wouldn't be the first time a boat was taken by pirates. But chopping off arms isn't their thing. Usually, it's just a bullet to the head and a shove over the transom."

Jimmy used to be my first mate, but now he works for a fly fishing school for kids. He still mates for me from time to time, though. Not that I really needed a mate, since I'd cut back so much on charters. A couple of decades younger than me and Rusty, Jimmy was very wise and in tune with everything around him. He claimed to have an old soul.

"Doc said he'd call me if he learned anything more. Outside of what I already told you, that's pretty much it."

"This the weekend that Kim's coming home?" Rusty asked.

"No, Marty's probably headed up there right now. The arm caused him to get a late start."

"Then that ain't his pickup pulling into the lot?" Rusty asked, nodding toward the window.

Turning on my stool, I looked outside to see Marty climbing out of his Dodge pickup. He was still in uniform and came straight to the door. He paused just inside, taking off his sunglasses.

"Thought you'd be halfway to Miami by now," I said as he crossed over to the bar.

"Change of plans. The sheriff assigned me the arm case and now I'm working the weekend."

"That's a good thing, right?" Rusty asked.

"I guess so," Marty replied, sitting down next to me and accepting the bottle of water from Rusty. "At least, it would be if I could find out who the guy was and who did it. I mean, there's little chance of that, with nothing but an arm to go on. At least he authorized overtime. That never hurts. Kim said she'd come down here instead. Should be here in less than an hour."

"Anything come back on the guy's prints, man?" Jimmy asked.

"Nothing, but IAFIS computers are sometimes slow." IAFIS is the FBI's Integrated Automated Fingerprint Identification System, a vast network of computers that store criminal fingerprints and can match them a million times faster than by eye.

"So, if you're working this weekend, why's Kim coming here?" I asked. "Not that I don't want to see my daughter, but you guys seem to have worked out a schedule."

Marty grinned, uncomfortably. He still wasn't at ease talking about his relationship with my youngest daughter. But, Kim's eighteen now and he's only a couple of years older.

"Yeah, she likes things scheduled," he said. "I think she's more concerned, because it was you that found the arm, though."

Just then the door opened and we all turned toward it. Seeing Linda's figure silhouetted against the still-bright afternoon sun, I rose and met her halfway.

"Why is it always such a chore to get out of Miami on a Friday?" she asked, wrapping her arms around my neck and kissing me deeply.

I took Linda's hand and led her to the bar, where Rusty already had a cold Michelob Ultra on a coaster for her. "'Cause everyone and their grandma wants to get outta there," he said. "Good to see ya again, Agent Rosales."

Linda smiled at Rusty. "So very nice to see you as well, Mister Thurman."

Jimmy and Marty both shifted over a stool, allowing Linda room next to me at the end of the bar. "What are you doing here in uniform, Marty?" Linda asked as she slid onto the stool. "Shouldn't you be in Gainesville this weekend?"

"I found an arm out on Harbor Channel this morning," I said. "Marty's been assigned the case."

She turned her head quickly toward me, tossing her auburn brown hair over her shoulder, concern in her dark smoky eyes. "You found an arm?"

"What was left of one, anyway," I replied. "The coroner suspects murder, said it was cut off with a chain saw."

Though she was a seasoned special agent for the state's top law enforcement agency, she visibly shuddered, but quickly gathered herself and turned to Marty. "An arm from a John Doe? Any leads?"

"Nothing yet," the young deputy replied. "I think the sheriff only gave me the case because none of the investigators wanted it. Hard to find out whodunit if you don't have a whole body."

"True," she said, "but if you do, it'd be a big step up for your career."

"Think so?" Marty asked.

"Absolutely. If I can help in any way, just ask. In fact, I met a woman up in Tallahassee who is doing forensic research on this very subject. I'm sure she'd love to come down, consult with you and examine the limb. Want me to call her?"

"I don't have the authority to hire outsiders," Marty said.

"I doubt you'd have to. She's flown all over the country on her own dime to research dismemberment cases."

"Doc Fredric seems pretty sure it was a chain saw," I offered.

"He's good, but I bet this woman could tell what kind of chain saw was used and if the person who did it was right- or left-handed. And if you ever locate the saw, she could match the tool marks in the blade to the bone, at a microscopic level, and say for certain it was or wasn't that particular saw."

"They can do that?" Marty asked.

"Sure," Linda replied. "There was a time that matching a bullet to a specific gun was considered hokey science."

The door opened again and it was Marty's turn to meet Kim halfway. They hugged and joined us at the bar, where Kim gave me a quick peck on the cheek. "Think you can keep my boyfriend away from me by getting him involved in a murder case, Dad?"

I raised both hands defensively. "Whoa, now. I'm not the sheriff."

"I'm just messing with you," she said with a wink and a punch to the shoulder. "I know you like Marty."

Kim saying that seemed to please the young man. "We'll have a little time. The sheriff won't make me work too many hours."

Linda looked back toward me and asked, "So what's on the agenda for the weekend?"

"Why don't we all go fishing?" I suggested. "The *Revenge* hasn't been away from the dock in two weeks. You busy, Jimmy?"

"Not a bit, dude. We just graduated a class the other day, and the next one's not due to start until Monday. I can get all my stuff ready for it on Sunday."

"I'm meeting Doc Fredric in an hour," Marty said. "Then I'll be busy all day tomorrow, checking missing persons all across the state. Hopefully he can help ID the guy."

"I'll go," Kim said to me. "If Marty's gonna be working, I want to fish."

The others laughed and Rusty said, "At least one apple didn't roll far. Count me in, too. Rufus can handle things here for half a day."

Rufus is Rusty's chef. An older guy, maybe mid- to late sixties, nobody really knows for sure. Once you start talking to him, it just feels unseemly to ask. Several years ago, just after his wife passed away, he'd retired from his job as the head chef of a five-star resort on his home island of Jamaica. He'd spent part of his youth here in the Keys and returned about the same time I retired from the Marine Corps and came here to live.

Finishing her beer, Linda declined another. "Are we ready?" she asked, standing up. "I'm anxious to get away from civilization."

Kim rose and gave Marty a quick kiss. "Me too. But you'll be out later this evening?"

Marty glanced at me and I gave him a slight nod. He smiled and rose from his stool, giving her a quick hug. "Sure, Kim. I'll see you then."

As he started for the door, Linda said, "I'll get in touch with my forensics friend and have her call you."

Standing up, I said to Rusty and Jimmy, "About zero seven hundred?"

"You got it, bro. We can have breakfast here before we head out on the blue."

"See ya in the morning, dude," Jimmy replied.

As Marty made his way to his pickup, the three of us went down to the dock, untied the *Knot L-8*, and climbed aboard. Carl and I had built her last winter and spring. All wood and a throwback design, with two big inboard V-twin engines for power, she turned heads everywhere.

All three of us got in the forward cockpit and I started the engines. We'd found that she was actually more economical to operate than either Carl's Grady-White or my big Winter center console, and she could run circles around either. More efficient as a people mover, anyway. What she lacked in cargo-carrying capacity, she more than made up for in looks. I shoved the bow away from the dock and engaged the transmissions.

"Where's Pescador?" Linda asked as we idled down the canal toward open water.

"He's been acting kinda down lately," I replied. Pescador's my big Portuguese water dog. I'd found him over two years ago, stranded on an island after a hurricane. "Seems like just playing with Carl and Charlie's kids for a short while wears him out and all he wants to do is sleep."

"Well, in dog years, he's probably close to forty," Kim said. "Everyone slows down a little at that age."

Passing the end of the canal, I said, "Ha! Speak for yourself, kiddo." I pushed the foot throttle halfway and the big motorcycle engines roared, lifting the boat up on plane almost instantly.

*Knot L-8* is a great little boat. She has strong oak ribs, overlaid with western red cedar on the hull and mahogany and teak on the fore and aft decks, then a thin skin of fiberglass and epoxy. It's the aft section that's most notable. Carl and I built her with a barrel-back design, the rear deck and engine compartment hatch sloping down from the rear cockpit and the gunwales flaring inboard. The aft section is about all that other boaters see of her, as she's quite capable of reaching seventy knots or more on calm water.

I kept the speed down in the small swells of the Atlantic, while Linda made a phone call. She ended the call just as we reached the Seven Mile Bridge and the calmer waters to the north of it. Turning left and paralleling traffic moving across the bridge, I opened the big motorcycle engines up and we were soon skimming across the glassy sheltered water, passing the cars on the bridge like they were standing still.

Looking over at Kim and Linda, I saw that both were smiling, their hair flying back wildly in the slipstream. Linda lifted her face to the warm sun, now halfway to the horizon, and said loud enough to be heard over the engines, "It's always good to come back down here. Sometimes I wonder why I stay on with the department."

"Why do you do it, then?" Kim asked, glancing over.

Linda thought on it a moment. "Someone has to, and I'm pretty good at what I do."

"Then just teach someone to do it and quit," Kim said. "When I finish college, I'm coming down here to stay."

That was a revelation to me. I knew Kim loved the water and enjoyed coming down here. "Really?"

Facing me, Kim got that serious look on her face, like she did when she tried to straighten me out on how to run the charter business. "I changed my major, Dad."

Kim had started college at the beginning of the summer, intent on getting a head start and graduating with a degree in business in just three and a half years. Changing her mind on something wasn't like her. "You're not planning on a business degree?"

"No," she replied. "Nearly a third of the students at UF are majoring in business, and the job market's not all that great."

My first thought was that she was planning on something to do with the water. Maybe oceanography or marine biology. "What are you majoring in, then?"

"Criminal justice," Kim replied flatly. I nearly missed the turn into Spanish Harbor Channel.

# CHAPTER FOUR

J ust six miles up US-1 from the *Rusty Anchor*, Marty's phone rang as he pulled off the highway, tires crunching on the crushed-shell driveway to the medical examiner's office. When he answered, an English woman's voice on the other end asked if he was Deputy Phillips.

When he said that he was, she continued, "A friend called me just a moment ago, Deputy. Linda Rosales, with FDLE? This is Meg Stewart calling. I'm with Forensic Outreach of London."

"London? Linda said you were local."

"Well, I am, actually. I live in Orlando. Our company is branching out here in the United States. Linda told me you have a fresh limb from an unknown victim. Any chance it was a simple boating accident?"

"I'm on my way in to meet the chief medical examiner now, Mizz Stewart. But his initial finding on the scene this morning pointed toward homicide."

"Linda said a chain saw was used. Is that correct? Oh, and please, do call me Meg."

Pulling through the gate at the end of the shell road, Marty maneuvered his pickup into a parking spot and climbed out. "Then you'll have to call me Marty. Yeah, from Doc Fredric's early examination, he's pretty sure that it was a chain saw."

"May I please come have a look, Marty? My specialty is forensic anthropology, mutilation, and dismemberment. Our kerf analysis database is quite extensive. I can be there tonight and meet you and Doctor Fredric first thing in the morning, if that's convenient."

"We're a pretty small department, Meg. I'm not sure we can afford to hire an outside consultant."

"There'll be no cost at all, Marty. We're a privately funded organization. I'd really love to see your arm."

Reaching the door to the metal building, Marty stopped just outside, knowing that he'd lose his signal as soon as he walked in. "In that case, I'm sure Doc won't mind. Say eight o'clock?"

"That would be wonderful, Marty."

"I'm just about to walk into the morgue now. If Doc can't see you at eight, I'll call you right back with a time that he can. Otherwise, I'll see you at eight."

Meg said goodbye and Marty ended the call, walking through the heavy metal door. The woman had a pleasant voice, but Marty couldn't help but wonder how a woman had become involved in this particular kind of research. Or a man, for that matter.

Making his way quickly through the building, Marty soon arrived at the morgue. He'd only been here a half dozen times, but only twice since graduating from the academy. He pushed the call button next to the door and waited.

"Right on time, Marty," Doc Fredric's voice came over a speaker next to the button. The door buzzed and Marty pulled it open and walked inside.

"Hey, Doc. Busy day?"

"No, thankfully not," the old doctor replied. Rising from his desk, he walked between two gurneys, one empty and the other occupied by a corpse, with a sheet pulled over it. "Come over here. I'll show you what I found out."

Pulling open one of the six small rectangular doors on the back wall, Doc pulled out a full-sized cadaver tray. The arm looked as out of place there as it had on the casting deck of Jesse's boat.

"Do you know a lady by the name of Meg Stewart, Doc? She's with a company out of London, called Forensic Outreach."

"Only by reputation, son. She's one of the leading specialists in kerf identification in the world. Why?"

Marty was already uncomfortable being in the morgue, and now he was even more so, thinking he might have overstepped his bounds.

"She'd like to examine the arm," Marty blurted out. "If it's okay with you, that is. She'll be here in the morning."

"Wonderful!" Doc said, poking him in the chest. "I like a young man with initiative, and I know the sheriff does as well. Unfortunately, I'll be in Key West. I was planning to transport the arm there, but since this is your investigation, I'll leave it here so you can let Miss Stewart examine it. Now have a look."

Handing Marty a large magnifying glass, he pointed to the end of the bone. "Remember my telling Jesse about the spur?"

Marty bent over the tray and held the glass close to the severed bone. Noting the position of the arm, he said, "Looks to be on the underside, where the triceps muscle is."

"Very good. Yes, it is. Remember my explaining to Jesse how a spur is usually on the end of the two-by-four that's resting on the sawhorses, as pressure is applied to the free end?"

"I've done my share of framing, Doc," Marty replied. "I know exactly what you mean."

"If you were to dismember someone with a chain saw, how would you do it?"

Marty straightened up and visibly shuddered. "Gives me the jitters just thinking about it. I guess that, using a chain saw, I'd just lay the body spread-eagle on the ground and saw away."

"That would be the easiest way, certainly. However, since the body is heavier than the arm, as the saw cuts through to the other side of the bone, that spur would be on the bone still attached to the body, would it not?"

Looking down at the floor, Marty considered what the doctor had said. "Yeah, I suppose you're right. And the spur would probably be on the side of the bone, either the front side or the back side, depending on whether you were standing over the body or the head."

Grinning broadly, the doctor stretched his arms out to either side. "What if the person weren't lying on the ground?"

"But, wouldn't the spur still be on the body side?"

"Allow me to demonstrate," Doc said, walking around the cadaver tray. "May I hold your arm?"

Marty nodded and the doctor lifted his arm, holding it by the wrist with one hand, Marty's hand resting on his shoulder. Doc pushed up on the underside of his elbow to straighten it. "The person was held up, like this. Probably by two people, one on either side, so that the arms were what was supported, not the man."

"Kinda dangerous, Doc. I mean, trying to hold up a grown man's body, that's a lotta dead weight."

Lowering Marty's arm, the doctor looked up at the young deputy and smiled, letting him come to the only conclusion that made sense in his own time.

It became suddenly clear to Marty. "This guy was alive when they chopped his arm off?"

"I believe he was, yes. You have a pretty sharp mind, son. I do believe you're going to crack this case."

After collecting the doctor's report, Marty waited while Doc made arrangements for him and Meg Stewart to be allowed access to the morgue in the morning.

Leaving the building, he got in his pickup and headed south on US-1 toward the sheriff's department substation. Parking behind the building, he went inside and made his way to his captain's office. He knocked on the open door frame, anxious to tell Captain Brian Hammonds what he'd learned.

"Come in, Marty. What was the ME's finding?"

Marty entered the small office and handed the captain the official coroner's report. "Doc says it was definitely a homicide, sir."

Hammonds' brow furrowed as he took the report and quickly flipped the pages. "Homicide? How can he tell that just from a severed limb?"

"From the location of the bone spur at the end of the cut. Doc says the dismemberment was likely the cause of death." Marty stretched his arms out wide. "The victim was being supported in a standing position when the arm was hacked off with a chain saw."

"Good Lord," Hammonds muttered, quickly crossing himself. He handed the report back to Marty. "It's your assignment, son. I bet a few of the homicide dicks will want to take it from you when this gets out, but it's yours until the sheriff says otherwise. Need any help?"

Marty couldn't suppress his grin. "Not right now, sir. I'm meeting a forensic anthropologist in the morning. She specializes in dismemberment and kerf identification."

"Kerf?"

"The cuts made from tools on bone," Marty replied, puffing up just a little.

Standing up, Hammonds came around the desk and stood looking up at the tall young deputy. "You do know you're not authorized to outlay funds for consults without approval, right? But, in this case, I'll let it slide if this woman can come up with a lead. If not, the cost will come outta your salary."

Grinning, Marty said, "No problem, Captain. She does pro bono research. I'm meeting her at the morgue in the morning."

Hammonds placed a hand on Marty's shoulder, turning him to the door. "Good. You keep me posted on what's happening. And I want a copy of her report, alright?"

Turning and walking toward the door, Marty told the captain he would and then started to leave the office.

He stopped in the doorway and turned around. "Captain, this forensic anthropologist woman is supposed to be the top in her field. Okay if I put her up at the Sombrero Resort?"

"Sure, son," Captain Hammonds replied. "But it's on your dime if she doesn't have anything to contribute. The department can't afford to pay the way for specialists, just so they can add to their database."

"Thank you, sir," Marty replied and turned down the hall toward the parking lot.

It was a short drive to the hotel, where he put a standard room on his expense card. Outside, he pulled up the woman's number on his phone's memory and called her back.

When Meg answered, Marty said, "I made arrangements at Sombrero Resort for a room. It's just a few miles from the morgue. I can pick you up, if you'd like."

"Thanks, Marty," Meg replied. "A resort, though?"

"The department has it covered," he lied. "And it's just called a resort because it's on the water and has a marina. There are more expensive places in town, but Sombrero's pretty nice, and it's where we usually house consultants. Mostly, it's convenient. They have their own marina, and I work mostly on the water."

"Alright, then," she replied. "I'm not very good at finding my way around strange places."

"Right next door to the resort is a place called Dockside. They serve breakfast and I can meet you there at eight, if that works for you."

"That would be lovely," she replied. "How do I find this resort?"

"Simple," Marty said. "Get on US-1 up in Homestead, and about eighty miles later you'll come into Marathon. Stay on US-1 past the airport and turn left just after the Kmart. Go just a few hundred feet and turn right on Sombrero Boulevard. It's about half a mile on the right. You can't miss it."

She thanked him again and Marty ended the call, climbing into his pickup. Driving the short distance to City Marina, just on the other side of the hospital, he thought over what Doc Fredric had said. He couldn't think of a more terrifying way to die than being hacked up with a chain saw.

# CHAPTER FIVE

**W**hat's this?" Agent Dave Parsons asked when his office manager, Sergeant First Class Mike Cooper, placed a file in his empty inbox.

"A civilian missing person's report, sir. File says 'eyes only,' so I figured I'd let you open it."

"Dammit! I'm only a couple months from mandatory retirement," the CID special agent in charge grumbled. "And what the hell is Criminal Intelligence investigating a missing civilian for?"

Sergeant Cooper merely shrugged and started to leave. "Wait, Mike," Parsons said. The younger soldier stopped in the doorway and turned around. "Sorry, I didn't mean to snap. I just about have this fraud case wrapped up and it's got me a bit on edge. I should be starting to check out, not digging into another investigation."

"The Army machine is kinda blind as well as ponderous, sir. Want me to have the courier wait?"

"Won't matter, will it?"

Cooper had been posted here just before Parsons, in charge of the daily managing of the office, controlling the handling and movement of both evidence and paperwork.

"Probably not," Cooper replied. "Between us we have almost half a century in the Army, and even coming here from two different fields, some things are pretty much the same."

"That'll be all," Parsons said, dismissing the sergeant and picking up the file.

Dave Parsons had joined the Army nearly thirty years ago, fresh out of high school and a summer filled with partying in Montgomery, Alabama. He'd enjoyed the early years of Army life and reenlisted in 1981 for a chance to make a lateral move to Military Police. As an MP, he'd excelled in his job and moved up in rank.

Almost seven years after enlisting, he'd finished the associate's degree program in criminal justice as a twenty-five-year-old sergeant. On the short list for staff sergeant, Parsons was instead transferred to Fort Leavenworth, Kansas, to attend the Army's Warrant Officer School.

Graduating from there, the newly appointed WO1 was shipped to Germany, where he worked in foreign intelligence and traveled all over the world. That had ended with this last posting. But for the four previous years, CWO4 Parsons had been a federal agent with the Army's Criminal Investigation Division, primarily investigating stateside murder cases involving active-duty Army personnel.

However, nearing mandatory retirement after twenty-nine years of service, he'd been transferred to the fraud division and assigned as special agent in charge of this small office in Melbourne, Florida. He never saw it as a demotion, as others who had handled high-profile cases might. It was the Army's way of winding a man down toward the end of a career. A few general-grade officers and sergeants major stay beyond thirty years, but that wasn't usually an option in the warrant officer and lower enlisted ranks. He'd done what the Army had asked of him, knew his track record was good, and he was enjoying the slower-paced job of assigning cases to the other agents that worked under him.

Aside from an occasional case or problem that came up when the other agents were fully engaged with their own assignments, Parsons handled very few himself. With his retirement looming at the end of the year, his case load became even lighter. Taking on a case that might take months was out of the question. He'd only have to bring someone else up to speed to take it over. Although it put more work on the other agents, it really was the only way, and he felt guilty for the free time he had.

He'd decided he liked the Melbourne area and wanted to make it his retirement hometown. He'd bought a townhouse overlooking a man-made lake in the North Melbourne suburb of Suntree. It was so close, he could look across Wickham Road from his office window and see the rooftops of the townhouses at the end of his street, peeking above the ten-foot-high wall that blocked the traffic noise.

Parsons thumbed through the missing person file. A man a few years older than himself by the name of Darius Minnich had gone missing. Also missing were his much younger and very attractive wife, Celia Minnich, and their crew. They had been reported overdue just yesterday, when the CFO of his company had contacted Dade County Police. The couple hadn't returned from a cruise on his luxury yacht, *Obsession*, and repeated phone calls went unanswered.

It wasn't until Parsons read further in the man's bio that he finally saw the connection to the Army. Minnich owned a high-tech company that had received a DoD contract to develop a new type of sniper's ghillie suit, using dozens of fiber-optic cameras that would render a stationary wearer virtually undetectable.

"A Predator suit?" Parsons mumbled to himself, thinking of the Schwarzenegger movie. In it, an alien wore a suit that projected images from one side onto the other, making him almost invisible.

Just then, Parsons's intercom buzzed. He pushed the button and said, "What is it, Mike?"

"A Colonel Brash on line two, Mister Parsons."

Without acknowledging, Parsons picked up the phone on his desk and pushed the flashing button for the call on hold. "SAC Parsons."

"This is Colonel Walter Brash at the Pentagon, Mister Parsons."

Knowing that Army couriers used electronic scanners to transmit delivery information, and quickly putting two and two together, Parsons knew why the colonel was calling.

"I've only just started to read the bio on the missing couple, Colonel."

"I'm sending two MPs from Lakeland. They'll meet you in the morning at the offices of CephaloTech in Miami. You're instructed to handle this case personally."

"Contact?"

"The company's chief operating officer is a woman by the name of Delores Juarez. Are you familiar with Air Force General Clyde Bottoms?"

"Assistant Secretary for Army Acquisitions?"

"Correct," the colonel replied. "CephaloTech has been working on a project for the last six years, a pet project of General Bottoms. It was he that specifically requested you handle this. The CephaloTech project has gone through initial testing with the 197th at Benning and MARSOC at Lejeune. It's supposed to be exhibited at a joint services demonstration in less than a month."

"Is the COO a suspect in the disappearance?"

"That's for you to find out, Agent Parsons."

"I'm leaving in five minutes," Parsons said as his cellphone vibrated in his pocket. "To whom do I report, sir?"

"Report directly to me. My adjutant just sent my contact information to your encrypted sat phone. Use only that to send information. This investigation is top secret. The MPs meeting you are for manpower only."

"Roger that, Colonel. Anything else?"

"I'm being fed information slowly, Agent Parsons. What I get and when I get it, I'll forward to your email."

The line went dead, and Parsons buzzed Cooper in the outer office. "Get in here, Mike."

When Cooper came in, Parsons tossed him a set of keys and put the Minnich file in his briefcase, snapping it shut.

"Lock up and go home, Mike. I'll be out of the office for at least the weekend, and the other agents are in the field. Forward the phones to your cell when you leave. If anything comes up on that fraud case, you handle it."

"Me, Mister Parsons?"

"Who the hell else? We're short-staffed, and the Pentagon has ordered me to handle this case personally. You know everything going on here and you're more than capable enough."

"Thanks, sir. But wouldn't that be a bit unorthodox? I'm not an investigator. I'm a paper pusher."

"That might be your MOS, Mike, but you'd have made a good investigator. Don't worry, the investigation is all but wrapped up. Just waiting for all the pieces to fall into place."

"I'll do what needs to be done, Mister Parsons. Where are you going?"

"This missing person's case involves a company out of Miami with a DoD contract. The Pentagon wants me to handle it, so that'll be my first stop. I'll call you on Monday, if I'm not back here already."

Lifting the briefcase, Parsons opened the storage closet where they kept printer paper and staples, picked up the go bag he always kept there, and headed out to the parking lot. Five minutes later, he pulled into the driveway of his townhouse.

Never married, Parsons's home was much larger than he needed. In the past, he'd lived on post, or rented a small one-bedroom apartment near wherever he'd been assigned. He'd heard about this townhouse coming on the market shortly after deciding to retire in Melbourne and had approached the owner. The guy was ecstatic that he wouldn't have to pay a realtor commission and agreed to the offer Parsons had made him. They'd closed the next week and Parsons had paid cash for the three-bedroom townhouse.

Quickly packing a few other essentials, he went to his closet, took a garment bag containing a cleaned and pressed suit and laid it out on his bed. His go bag contained coveralls, a CID windbreaker, body armor, a backup Colt revolver in an ankle holster, and dozens of investigative tools and materials.

Ten minutes later, Parsons was taking the ramp from Wickham Road to Interstate 95. Merging with the usual slow-moving traffic headed south, he moved to the left lane and brought the big blue Ford sedan up to eighty miles per hour, then set the cruise control. Checking his watch as he passed the one eighty-nine mile marker, he estimated he'd be in Miami by midafternoon. Early enough to catch the head of the company's operations before she went home for the day. A part of him hoped she'd be eligible for overtime, since his interviews were usually lengthy.

# CHAPTER SIX

Arriving back at the island, I clicked the key fob, and the doors on the east side of the dock area started to swing open as we tied *Knot L-8* off to the pier. Kim wanted to take her skiff out while she was home, and I'd have to juggle some boats around. So I sent her and Linda ahead while I stood staring through the open doors at the boats.

The west side of the dock area held the two larger boats, the forty-five-foot *Revenge* and the forty-two-foot Cigarette. No room there to swing a cat.

The east side was crowded with five boats, but there might be a way to creatively get everything under cover and not have to use the hoist. The idea of leaving any boat tied to the pier for more than a few hours just didn't cut it in my mind.

Kim's skiff was back in the corner, in the hoist above mine. With nearly fifty feet between the rear catwalk and the door, I knew it'd be tight, but one of the eighteen-foot Maverick skiffs could be docked in front of the thirty-foot *Cazador*. If they were docked bow to bow, there would be just enough room to close the door without crushing the outboard.

The skiff rode much lower and was less beamy than the big Winter inboard. We rarely used *Cazador* anymore, unless we had to move a lot of stuff. For that, it was perfect. I'd been docking *Knot L-8* in front of my skiff since I'd found I liked using her a lot more. The twenty-foot Grady-White was docked with her stern to the rear catwalk, between my skiff and *Cazador*.

All this meant not having direct egress for my skiff or *Cazador*, but they were rarely used, so that's how things would be. At least when Kim was here. She'd really fallen in love with the little Maverick Mirage, just as my late wife had. Sometimes, Kim would spend hours out on the flats to the west, just poling around and exploring.

It didn't take long to move my skiff out of the way and lower hers, then swing it around in front of *Cazador*. As I was backing my skiff into the corner, Kim came out on the dock and stood watching, Pescador sitting beside her.

"Start her up and back her in right there in front of me," I called out to her.

"Me? You want me to back your boat in?"

"You or Pescador," I replied with a grin. "She maneuvers just like the *Revenge*. Just a lot more responsive."

Kim climbed into the wooden boat and started the engines before casting off and shoving the bow away from the pier. Pescador jumped into the forward cockpit at the last minute.

Allowing the boat time to slowly drift out into the small turning basin, she engaged the two engines in opposite directions and *Knot L-8* continued spinning.

A moment later, she had her backed in and Pescador jumped out and sat beside me for an ear scratch.

"I can feel the power of those engines through the wood," Kim remarked, making small talk as she climbed out.

There hadn't been any more discussion about her change in majors since she'd blurted it out on the way home. I wasn't sure how I felt about it. Criminal justice could lead to law school. *My daughter, the lawyer*, I thought. But I felt pretty certain that wasn't going to be the case.

"Yep," I simply replied as I knelt to tie off the bowline. I knew she wanted to talk and just let her get her thoughts sorted.

After tying off the stern, Kim stood up and looked at me a moment before speaking. "Linda suggested I come give you a hand. Guess that was some big news I just dumped on you, huh?"

I just shrugged, letting her come to what she wanted to say in her own time. "I want to do what you, Linda, and Marty do. That's not so bad, is it?"

"What I do is run a charter business."

"You know what I mean, Dad."

I looked up at her as I finished tying off the bowline. "What Linda and Marty do, I might go along with," I said. "But not what I do."

"You make people around you feel safe. All three of you. Deuce and Julie, too. I don't mean all the secret stuff y'all do. More like what Marty does, if that makes sense."

"You want to be a cop." I said it as a statement, forcing her to confirm or deny it.

She looked down at the catwalk for a moment and kicked at a small bit of sand there. Finally, she looked up at me and put her hands on her hips. "Fish and Wildlife."

"Marine Patrol?"

"They're not called that anymore, Dad."

"I know," I said with a sigh. "You just have such a good head for business, that's all."

"I don't see myself as cubicle material. Busting my butt for someone else, waiting for someone to retire or die, before I could move up the corporate ladder."

"Not all business is done in cubicles and offices," I said.

"But business people don't help others. Not the way Linda does. They don't draw a line and stand on it, keeping those that would do harm away from people just trying to live their lives."

"Linda? I thought this was about you and Marty."

"Maybe some," Kim said. "But all those weekends last spring, when Linda came down and y'all talked about her work? She's really an amazing woman."

I couldn't suppress a chuckle. "You won't get any argument from me on that."

"Take that phone call she made on the way up here," Kim said, heading to the door. "Sure, that forensics lady will probably be a big help in Marty's investigation, but that's not why Linda did it. She's like you. Both of you have a deep-rooted need to see that justice is served. You just go about it in different ways. I think I have that need, too. That's all."

I clicked the lock button on the key fob, the twelve-volt motor actuating to pull the doors closed, and followed my daughter up the steps to the deck. Pescador bounded ahead of us, going straight to Linda, sitting at the table with Charlie.

I see an awful lot of myself in my youngest daughter. She loves the outdoors, especially the water, and she'd taken to the island and boating lifestyle like a duck to water. As for her morals and motivation, I really feel she follows the same compass that I do.

"What about your scholarships?" I asked as we both sat down with Linda and Charlie. "Are they transferable to this new major?"

"Well, no, not exactly," Kim replied, taking two bottles of water from a cooler by the table and handing me one. "That's something I need to talk to you about. Hi, Charlie."

"Nice to see you again," Charlie said. "Linda was just telling me about your changing majors. Congratulations."

"It's not final yet," I said.

Kim stared straight into my eyes and said, "Yeah, Dad. It is."

Looking back at her, I saw one of my own not-so-virtuous qualities looking back. When Kim set her mind to something, she could be more stubborn than an old Missouri mule.

I accepted the defeat the only way I could. Capitulate and negotiate a better outcome. "Okay, I'll pay for the tuition and books. On one condition."

Linda smiled and gave me a look of commiseration. She had a son who was a senior at UF.

"What's the condition?" Kim asked.

"A three point eight grade point average. Drop below that and I'll turn off the faucet."

Kim glanced quickly at Linda, who very inconspicuously winked back. "Deal," Kim said as she turned back to face me and extended her hand. I bypassed the handshake and gave her a hug instead.

Just then, I heard Linda's cellphone ring. She prefers that annoying, high-pitched old-style telephone ringer for a ringtone. She slid the phone out of the pocket of her jeans and answered it. A moment later she smiled and said, "Yeah, he's right here." Extending the phone to me, she said, "For you. It's Deuce."

Deuce Livingston is one of my closest friends. His dad, Russ, had been my platoon sergeant way back in the eighties, when Rusty and I were stationed together in Okinawa, Japan. Deuce also happens to be married to Rusty's daughter, Julie.

Holding the phone to my ear, I spoke with feigned disdain. "What do you want, Squid?"

Deuce had the same hearty laugh and quick wit Russ had had. Unfortunately, he lacked his dad's strength of character and had ended up a Navy SEAL officer. The interservice rivalry game we played was all in fun. Fact is, Deuce is about the most capable and trustworthy man I've ever known.

"I was just telling Julie that we hadn't had fried grunts in a while and naturally I thought of you, you old worn-out Grunt."

"Har har. How're things in the Puzzle Palace?"

Deuce works at the Pentagon. A couple of years ago, he'd been assigned to head up a counterterrorism team, working out of Homestead. He was now the acting deputy director of Homeland Security's Caribbean Counterterrorism Command, with two teams under his control. He and Julie have been living in DC for several months now.

"We're coming home," he said by way of reply.

"Really? That's great news. I bet Julie's excited about the visit."

"Yes, I am," I heard Julie herself reply. "You're on speaker, Uncle Jesse. But it's not a visit. We're coming home. Packing tomorrow and leaving Sunday morning."

"Outstanding news, Jules. Why the sudden change? They finally find a suit to fill your position, Deuce?"

"The secretary talked Colonel Stockwell out of retirement, He just told me this morning, and I met with the colonel this afternoon. Turning everything back over to him tomorrow."

Colonel Travis Stockwell had actually always been the ADD. He'd stepped down a few months back, retiring after forty years of service. At least, that's the story the DC papers were given. He'd recommended me to take over the position, but that had been a complete nonstarter on so many levels. So, Deuce and Julie were ordered to Washington, he as acting deputy director.

The fact was, Travis worked as my part-time first mate, which gave him lots of free time. During that free time, he was flying all over the Caribbean, directing a young woman that he and the Homeland secretary had turned into an assassin. After I'd figured it out, Travis had disappeared.

Standing, I held up a finger to the others and walked to the top of the stairs at the far end of the deck. "Why do I get the impression that this isn't a social call?"

I heard a click and his voice became clearer. "Probably because you have very good intuitive powers," he replied. "You know the colonel's been living like a retiree, having a good time all over the Caribbean. He picked up word about a contingent of Russian black marketers, camped in the Cay Sal Bank."

"Big area, Deuce."

"That's why I want you to take us there."

Turning around, I looked back at the three women sitting at the table. They were talking animatedly, probably about Kim's plan to change majors.

"No chance," I said.

"You won't even hear me out?"

A part of me wanted to. The Cay Sal Bank is part of the Bahamas, but the closest land mass of any size is Cuba, just thirty miles to the south of the huge triangular-shaped bank. It was ringed with tiny cays, some completely submerged at high tide. Nobody lived on any of them, unless you count boat bums who anchor there for weeks or months at a time. One of the larger cays would be real convenient for black marketers to operate out of with impunity. The Cuban government encouraged black marketing of just about any kind.

"Be glad to take you out fishing or diving," I finally said. "But that's about it, man. Sorry."

He didn't say anything for a second. Then I heard Julie's voice in the background, but couldn't make out what she said.

"Alright," he said with a sigh. "I get it, and to be honest, I don't blame you. You have it good now and you deserve it."

"You're right, I do. I'm forty-six and only now settling down. I've reconnected with my kids, have a good woman I get to chase around the bunk from time to time, good friends, and a nice quiet life. I've been fighting bad guys for almost three decades, brother. I'm tired."

"Let's get together for a beer, then," Deuce said. "We're flying into Homestead, arriving just after noon on Sunday. Rusty doesn't know yet, Julie wants to surprise him."

"We'll be there," I said, grinning. "Want me to open up your Whitby so it can air out a little?"

"If you can do it on the sly, yeah. It's been closed up for too long. Hope the engine isn't seized up."

"Will do," I said, walking back to the others. "We'll see you Sunday afternoon."

He said goodbye, I ended the call and handed the phone back to Linda. "They're coming home?" she asked.

I nodded. "Yep. For good. Leaving Sunday morning. We're meeting them at the *Anchor* in the afternoon, but don't say anything to Rusty."

"He'll be thrilled," Charlie said, standing up. "I have to go get dinner ready."

Kim was on her feet quickly. "I'll give you a hand."

Once they were down the steps, I turned and started to ask Linda what sort of conspiracy was going on between her and Kim, but she spoke before I could get a word out.

"Don't be angry."

"Me? Angry? About what?"

"She called me last week and asked about scholarships for criminal justice majors. Even if she doesn't maintain your three point eight, her tuition is paid. As long as it stays above a three point oh."

"So my negotiations were for naught?"

Linda smiled. "I doubt you'll have to worry about that. I'd be surprised if she didn't make straight As. I'm sorry, Jesse. But she asked me not to say anything until she talked to you."

"She really looks up to you," I said.

"Me? I thought she was doing it to be closer to Marty."

Taking Linda's hand, I looked down at Kim and Charlie picking a few vegetables for supper. "She says you draw a line and stand on it to protect others."

Linda laughed. She has a hearty, infectious laugh. "She told me nearly the same thing about you. Only she said that you're the kind of man that draws the line behind where he's standing."

Following my gaze, she added, "We think our kids never notice what we do."

# CHAPTER SEVEN

I t was still dark when I woke. The smell of Costa Rican coffee was the first thing I noticed. Rusty kept me well stocked with a dark roast from a little farm called La Minita, way up in the Costa Rican mountains. The gentle rustle of the curtains as a light breeze stirred them was the second thing I noticed. I gently rolled out of my big bed, careful not to wake Linda, and quietly pulled open the top dresser drawer for a clean pair of boxers.

Looking out the south-facing window, I saw the stars glittering off the water all the way to the horizon, not a cloud to obscure them. Yet the breeze was out of the north. The easterly trades were so constant, whenever the wind changed direction, it meant weather approaching. The northerly breeze meant a low-pressure system was building over Cuba.

I was nearly to the bedroom hatch when I heard Linda softly mumble, "Bring me a cup?"

I turned around. In the dappled light, I saw her sitting up in the bed, propped on her elbows, naked except for the bedsheet tangled around her long, tanned legs. Her hair hung wild and loose on her shoulders. Feeling a stirring in my groin, I began to walk back to my bed.

She held a hand up. "Not without a mug in your hands."

I grinned and headed out to the galley. Pescador was waiting patiently by the door, and I let him out. As I filled two mugs, I heard the shower come on and hurried into the head, carrying them both. Linda was already in the shower, facing away from the stream of hot water, lifting her hair with both hands, rinsing it. Sliding the clear shower door open, I slipped off my boxer shorts and stepped into the shower in front of her.

I handed my lady one of the mugs, and we each sipped at the strong brew, looking at one another over the rims as the hot water splashed over her shoulders and traced little rivulets over her breasts, down her belly and over her wide hips.

"Mmm, I needed that," she said with a sparkle in her eyes.

I didn't try to disguise the lust I felt. We'd moved well past that marker many months ago. "Me too."

Taking her half-empty mug, I placed them both on the high shelf and took her in my arms. I backed her under the full force of the water and into the corner of the large shower stall, as we embraced passionately.

Thirty minutes later, dressed for a day on the water, we joined Kim and the Trent family at the big table for more coffee. The west side of the western bunkhouse is partitioned off and used as kind of an office. It has two sets of bunk beds and Kim stays there when she comes to visit.

"Kim said y'all are going offshore," Charlie said. "Breakfast before you leave?"

"No, thanks," I replied. "We're meeting Rusty and Jimmy for breakfast at the *Anchor*."

"Hope you catch some dolphin," Carl said. "Haven't had any in over a week."

"Exactly why we're going. Can you make a little room in the freezer?"

"No problem," Charlie replied.

Finishing our coffee, we said our goodbyes and started to leave. Pescador looked up at me expectantly. "You wanna go fishing today, buddy?"

He barked once, which I always assumed meant yes. "Well, let's get a move on."

Like he had been shot out of the proverbial cannon, Pescador charged across the clearing. Making a beeline toward the house and the docks beneath it at a dead run, he sent sand and leaves flying up from underneath his paws.

"Looks like he really wants to go," Linda said.

Ten minutes later, with the sky just beginning to turn purple, we idled out into Harbor Channel and turned northeast toward the light on Harbor Key Bank. I brought the big boat up on plane, and minutes later we turned east and then southeast.

While the *Revenge* is equipped with state-of-the-art electronics and navigation, I'd become less and less reliant on them over the years. I'd made this run from my island to Marathon so many times, it'd become second nature. Whether on the *Revenge* or one of the other boats, I usually kept at the same sedate speed. The turns in East Bahia Honda Channel were timed subconsciously, and now I only occasionally checked the sonar.

Being only a degree or so north of the Tropic of Cancer, a lot of the southern constellations are visible here. Before dawn, in fall and early winter, the Southern Cross is setting after its short arc across the southern sky. It was this constellation that I was now navigating by, keeping it about fifteen degrees off the starboard bow.

With the lights on the bridge turned off and only the faintest glow coming from the forward-scanning sonar, I relied more on the visual cues the stars provided, knowing that the sonar alert tone would sound if the water ahead became too skinny, or there was some new obstruction on the bottom.

The shallowest part of the channel was five feet at high tide, and it was just before the tide now. As long as we didn't stray too far out of the natural channel that sailors have used for hundreds of years, we'd have at least five feet under the keel, and the *Revenge* only needed four. Not a lot of room for error, but as long as the tide was high, I'd take this shortcut. Other than that, the channel was a fairly constant ten feet in depth and would take us straight to Moser Channel and the high arch of Seven Mile Bridge.

"More coffee?" Linda asked as we cruised across the five-foot shallows at Horseshoe Bank without incident.

I nodded, watching the sonar for anything on the bottom. As she filled my mug, the sonar showed the bottom dropping away once again as we entered the main part of the channel.

"This is your favorite time to be on the water, isn't it?" she asked, handing the mug back to me.

"Yeah, I guess it is," I replied. "The start of a new day, a fresh, clean slate."

"Mine too," Kim added. "Sunsets are pretty, but the dawn brings with it the chance to start all over and forget about the mistakes of the previous day."

I chuckled as we passed East Bahia Honda Key on our starboard side. "When did you become such a philosopher?"

When we arrived at the Anchor, Jimmy was already there. Rufus was out in his little open-air kitchen, cooking, and entertaining a few of the locals and liveaboards. Kim took our orders and went out the back door to tell Rufus, while Linda and I joined Jimmy at the bar.

While most people would look with disdain at eating breakfast at a bar in a boat-bum beer joint, the *Anchor* was different from most. Tucked back in the mangroves and the gumbo-limbo and banyan trees, completely invisible to cars passing by on Overseas Highway, it was a hangout for locals. A place to catch up on the goings-on around the islands, make plans for the future, or just be with friends that were as close as family.

Rusty placed two more mugs at the end of the bar and filled them with the same strong, black La Minita coffee. "You feel the wind this morning?" Rusty asked.

"I'm sure we'll be back before the storm gets here," I said.

"Storm?" Linda asked. "What storm?"

"Wind's outta the north this morning," Jimmy said, nursing his own coffee. "Sure sign of bad weather down south, man."

"I didn't hear anything about a storm," Linda proclaimed.

"Old Fidel," Jimmy mused, "he just never seems to share very much with us."

Minutes later, Kim came back in, balancing three plates loaded with omelets and fried potatoes. "Y'all go ahead," Rusty said. "Me and Jimmy already ate."

Linda and I joined Kim at a table. "Rufus said to give you this," Kim said and handed me a small vial. "He said it would dull your sense of smell for about an hour."

I took the vial and looked at it. There was a clear liquid inside, thick and clinging to the sides. Leaning over the plate in front of me, I inhaled deeply, savoring the spicy aroma. "Why wouldn't I want to smell this? What is it?"

"Janga and wild onion omelet," Kim replied. "He said the vial was for later, while we were out on the boat."

I shook my head and shoved the little bottle into my pocket as I dug into the omelet. "Sometimes I just don't get that guy."

Kim grinned. "He also said the janga were for Linda."

"Then why'd you give it to me?"

Linda elbowed me in the ribs. What Rufus calls janga are actually the freshwater crawfish we raise on the island. In Jamaica, freshwater crawfish are called janga and are considered an aphrodisiac.

"What?" I said as I looked from one to the other.

Kim grinned again and said, "His exact words were, 'Di gods of di cosmos smile upon your daddy and his lady. Dey tell Rufus to help di mon.'"

Linda nearly choked, trying to swallow a bite and stifle a laugh. She quickly brought her napkin to her mouth, and finally she said, "He doesn't need any help."

"TMI," Kim said, laughing.

We quickly finished breakfast as Rusty and Jimmy carried coolers down to the boat, loaded with baitfish, drinking water, and beer. When the three of us joined them, Jimmy already had the engines running and the sun was just beginning to peek above the mangroves to the southeast, not a cloud in sight.

As Kim and Linda climbed up to the bridge, Rusty and I cast off the lines and stepped aboard. "Take us out, Jimmy," I called up to him. Pescador took up his now-usual spot on the deck by the transom door as Rusty and I emptied the live bait into the bait wells and turned on the aerators. For a year, when Pescador first came to live with me, he'd always ridden on the foredeck, as if looking out for something. I figured he liked this new spot because he was getting older and a little less active.

Rusty and I joined the others on the bridge before we reached the end of the canal. Kim looked longingly at my airplane, sitting near the top of the boat ramp. "Can we do some flying this weekend?"

"I doubt we can today," I said. "I don't think we'll have good weather this afternoon."

Jimmy started to get up from the helm and I nodded to Kim. "Why don't you pilot us out to the Stream, kiddo?"

Before she could answer, I went forward and sat down next to Linda on the forward-facing bench seat, putting my feet up.

"Weather'll be fine for flying tomorrow," Rusty offered.

"Yeah, maybe we can stay over at the *Anchor* tonight and take *Island Hopper* up in the morning," I said. "Meeting a prospective client there in the afternoon, anyway."

*Island Hopper* is the name painted on the cowling of my 1953 deHavilland Beaver float plane. I'd bought her from a friend last year, when he'd decided to move back to Kentucky.

I felt the familiar surge of power as Kim throttled up and the big twin props pushed water out from under the stern, lifting the bow. In seconds, we were up on plane, heading due south. The light south wind carried a slight aroma on it. The smell of the tropical jungles of western Cuba.

In less than an hour, with the sun barely fifteen degrees above the horizon, we neared the swift-moving Gulf Stream. It carried warm water from the Gulf of Mexico through the narrow Florida Straits between the Keys and Cuba. Then the Stream turned north, carrying it all the way up the Eastern Seaboard. Off Nova Scotia, it turned east, carrying the warm water across the cold North Atlantic. England's mild weather is due to this movement of billions of gallons of warm tropical water.

Jimmy and Kim set up the outriggers and got the rods and reels ready. Within a few minutes of putting the bait in the water, Jimmy yelled, "Fish on!"

Kim was between him and the fighting chair, and Jimmy quickly took up the rod, set the hook, and handed it to her as she sat down in the chair.

Throttling back, I stood and put my back to the wheel as Linda leaned on the rail to my left to watch. "There he is!" Linda shouted, pointing astern as a big bull dolphin broke the surface fifty yards behind the boat and did a little tail dance across the water, trying to throw the hook from his mouth.

Kim needed no coaching, but Jimmy and Rusty both stood next to the chair, cheering her on as she fought the big fish. Pescador added barks of encouragement, while I used the throttles to keep the stern of the *Revenge* toward the fish.

The fight lasted fifteen minutes, but Kim finally had the big bull alongside, where Rusty was able to gaff it and pull it through the transom door. Most of the bright colors had already drained from the dolphin's skin.

Linda began to squeeze past me, her breasts crushing against my chest. "I better get down there, before she catches them all."

For the next three hours, everyone had a turn in the chair, and we boated seven good-sized dolphin and quite a few amberjack and king mackerel. Linda even caught a small white marlin, which we released.

As we were preparing to head back in, Rusty pointed off to starboard and said, "Wonder what they're doing?"

Where he was pointing, about a mile away to the north, lay a large luxury yacht on the edge of the Stream. Not the kind of boat to be fishing the Gulf Stream, it seemed as though it was adrift. I knew there were usually lines of sargassum floating along the edge of the Stream.

*Maybe they've fouled their water intakes*, I thought.

"I'll see if they need help," I said, reaching for the microphone of the VHF radio. Keying the mic, I spoke into it. "This is *MV Gaspar's Revenge*, hailing the seventy-foot yacht adrift off our starboard side. Do you need assistance?"

Having finished putting everything away, the others joined me and Kim on the bridge, Linda talking excitedly about the billfish. Pescador turned around a couple of times before settling himself by the transom door for the ride home. No reply came back from my hail. I lifted the seat cushion, took out a pair of binoculars, and trained them on the yacht.

"I don't see anyone on deck," I said. Taking the mic, I double-checked that I was on channel sixteen and hailed them again.

When I didn't receive a reply again, I turned to Linda, beside me at the helm. "Are you carrying?"

She nodded toward her purse, hanging on the backrest of the second seat. "Always."

Turning to my daughter, the only other person with the combination to my box under the master bunk, I said, "Kim, go below and bring me my Sig."

"You think there's trouble, Dad?"

"Probably not, kiddo," I replied. "But it looks like something's wrong, and you know I don't like to take chances."

"Bring two," Rusty said, stepping over to the rail.

Nodding to Kim, I saw her hurry down the ladder as I turned the *Revenge* toward the other boat. I throttled up, just enough to get up on the step. A moment later, Kim handed up not one but two large watertight Penn Reel boxes before climbing up the ladder.

Rusty opened one of the boxes and withdrew a Sig Sauer nine-millimeter semiautomatic handgun and a magazine. He racked the slide back to check that the chamber was empty, released it, and slid the magazine into the grip. He then handed it to me as I slowly started to throttle back. I took the Sig and quickly chambered a round, then slid it into the waistband of my cargo shorts.

Rusty took a second, identical handgun out of the box while Kim opened the second box and she and Jimmy both armed themselves with a third Sig and a Glock forty-caliber.

The yacht was a very expensive Italian-made Pershing 76. It appeared to be a few years older than the current models, but seemed to be meticulously maintained. As we idled toward the bow, which was facing north, I sounded the big air horn mounted on the roof and shifted to neutral. We all watched, Rusty using the binoculars.

"No movement on deck," Rusty said. "And I don't see nothing through any of the portholes."

Reengaging the transmissions, I steered around the port side, making my way to the yacht's stern and trying to stay clear of the sargassum floating on the surface. As I looked through the smoked glass, the only silhouettes I could make out were the backs of the two seats at the helm on the top deck. The long afterdeck appeared empty as well.

"Where is everyone?" Kim asked.

Suddenly, Pescador started barking as I began to spin the *Revenge* around. I wanted to have the bow pointed away from the yacht and the sargassum, in case anything happened, and have the stern toward it, in case they needed help.

I looked down in the cockpit, and Pescador was standing with his paws on the gunwale, barking repeatedly and wagging his tail, obviously very excited. He jumped up onto the side deck and went forward, still barking at the yacht.

"What's with him?" Jimmy asked.

"I'm not sure," I replied, backing toward the yacht's huge swim platform. "He's never acted like this before."

"Oh my God," Kim said as we came astern the big luxury yacht. "What's that smell?"

I got quickly to my feet, as did Rusty. "Kim, take the helm," I ordered. "Bring the starboard side up to their stern." Rusty was right behind me going down the ladder. The stench became stronger as Kim maneuvered the *Revenge* up to the stern of the other boat.

I knew that smell. In the early eighties, while stationed together in Okinawa, Japan, Rusty and I had taken a week's leave and visited Sumatra. A huge flower grows there called a *titan arum*. The petals can grow up to ten feet long, and it emits an odor unlike any other flower. Nothing in this world comes close to the smell of a corpse flower. Except of course, a decomposing human corpse. Or maybe more than one decomposing human corpse.

As we neared the stern, Rusty and I stood ready by the gunwale. Pescador came down the side deck, still barking and wagging his tail excitedly, like he sometimes did when everyone had been away from the island for a while and he was left alone.

Linda came down the ladder and joined us. "I told Jimmy to stay aboard with Kim," she said. "They'll move off to the side once we board. It might not be safe. Someone on board that yacht is dead."

Like a light switch, Pescador's demeanor changed when he caught scent of the smell. Up on the foredeck, he'd been out of the wind blowing over the yacht as I'd backed toward its stern. He suddenly stopped barking, the hair bristling on the back of his neck and shoulders. A low rumble emanated from deep in his chest.

Kim's words from Rufus rang in my ear, "*He said the vial was for later, while we were out on the boat.*"

Taking the vial from my pocket, I quickly removed the cap and dabbed some on the front of my shirt. Covering my face with my shirt, I inhaled deeply, trusting in the old Jamaican mystic. The liquid in the vial smelled of frangipani and bananas for a moment, then suddenly the scent disappeared.

When I took the shirt away from my face, the disgusting odor from the boat was gone, too. I handed the vial to Linda first. "Just wet your shirt tail with this and smell it," I said.

The massive swim platform of the yacht was awash. Water lapped at the second step on either side of a large hatch, inside which an inflatable boat or jet-ski was probably stored below the sun pad. Still several feet away, Pescador suddenly leapt the gunwale, landing in the water with a big splash. I started to yell at him, worried he might be crushed between the two boats, but his large webbed paws propelled him across the remaining few feet quickly, his big tail acting as a rudder. In seconds, he was already at the steps of the yacht.

"She's riding low, Jesse," Rusty said, stating the obvious. "We better be careful, in case she rolls or starts to go down."

I was first over the gunwale, splashing onto the swim platform with water up to my midcalf. Drawing my Sig, I started up the port-side steps to the sundeck, following Pescador.

As I reached the sundeck, what I saw brought my senses and instincts to full alert. Dried, congealed blood was all over the sundeck and the huge padded lounge area. It had dripped down the sides of the elevated pad, pooling in the cracks of the personal watercraft hatch and on the polished mahogany deck itself. But there was no body.

Pescador was at the large smoked-glass door, standing on his hind legs and scratching at the handle with abandon. "Dear Lord," Linda said, reaching me on the sundeck. "What in hell happened here?"

Careful not to step in blood, which was difficult, I made my way to Pescador, who'd not bothered avoiding the blood and was leaving bloody paw prints and streaks on the glass door. His barking and low growl were gone. Now, he was nearly whimpering, anxious to get inside.

"Down, Pescador. Let me go first."

He seemed to calm a little and sat down by the door. I slid it open quickly, rushing through with my Sig leading the way and sweeping the interior. Pescador flashed past me, charging through the elegantly appointed, but totally trashed salon area, leaping over upturned chairs and seat cushions.

"Pescador, no!" I shouted after him, but he'd disappeared beyond a large-screen TV which separated the salon from the pilothouse.

Chasing after him, I saw that he'd disappeared down a set of steps on the starboard side. I went after him and found him in the forward stateroom, sniffing around the body of a partially nude woman, her body bloated in death.

The short black dress the woman wore was pulled up over her hips and the top was ripped and pulled down. The woman's head and arms were hanging off the side of the large bed. A pool of blood was directly below her head, already dried and congealed around a pile of her long dark hair. More blood and what appeared to be brain tissue were splattered on the port bulkhead above her head, with strands of dark hair matted to the mess.

On the starboard side of the stateroom, a man's body sat upright on a curved sofa. His feet were tied and his hands were behind his back, probably also tied. He was dressed in cruising casual clothes. The man also had dark hair, but graying a little at the temples. His head lay back over the small sofa, as if he'd dozed off. The hole in the center of his forehead, his bloated neck, and his tongue, swollen and protruding from his open mouth, told me that a nap wasn't the case. Even more blood and brain matter were splattered against the white padded bulkhead behind him, like some kind of gruesome New Age painting.

Pescador whined and disappeared back through the hatch, tearing down the companionway, where he almost knocked Linda over as he lunged for a closed hatch to another stateroom. Bouncing off the hatch, he was immediately up on his hind legs, scratching at the latch.

There were two other hatches off the companionway, both open. I pointed to Linda, then the port-side stateroom, across from me. As she covered the hatch to port, I stayed close to the bulkhead and quickly peered inside the stateroom on the starboard side.

Seeing nothing, I nodded to Linda. As I covered the remaining hatch with my Sig, she quickly peeked inside and withdrew, before stepping into the cabin, leading with her Beretta. A moment later, she came out and shook her head.

We both moved to where Pescador continued jumping at the master stateroom hatch, whimpering. "Get back, boy," I whispered. "And this time I mean it. Let me go first."

Pescador stepped out of the way and I tried the latch. It wasn't locked. Flinging it open, I stepped quickly inside. It didn't appear to be disturbed in any way. Linda was right on my heels, followed by Pescador, who immediately jumped onto the bed, his huge tail wagging crazily as he sniffed around the disheveled covers.

"Two dead in the forward stateroom," I told Linda as I opened the door to the private head and looked inside. Nothing out of place there, either. Glancing back at Linda, I added, "A man and a woman, both shot in the head, execution style."

Suddenly, a whirring noise came from below our feet and the sound of rushing water could be heard from outside the hull. "Sounds like Rusty found the switch for the bilge pumps," Linda said.

From outside the boat, I heard Kim scream.

"Jesse!" Rusty shouted from above. "Get up here, quick!"

Pescador was sniffing all over the room, but, sensing the urgency in Rusty's voice, he ran past us and up the ladder well to the salon. Following him, I saw Rusty on the sundeck, motioning us. "Out here!"

Next to the sliding glass door was another set of steps, which I assumed went down to the galley and crew quarters. We went quickly to where Rusty stood by the rail, looking down at the water. I followed his gaze and saw a severed leg, floating near the jet of water coming from the bilge pump, just below the waterline.

"Galley's below us," Rusty said. "Crew quarters, too. Nothing there, so I checked the engine room. Somebody pulled the bilge pump hose off the through-hull and disabled the pump. I reconnected the hose and turned on the pump, then came up here. Looks like that leg just happened to be floatin' by and got sucked up to the through-hull, blocking it from taking in more water."

"There's two bodies in the forward stateroom," I told him.

Rusty glanced at me. "Either one missing a leg?"

"No," I replied with a shudder. The leg was floating, thanks to an air pocket in the knee area of the uniform trousers. The shod foot and upper thigh dangled below the knee, which was bent almost ninety degrees.

Kim was holding the *Revenge* twenty feet off the port side. Standing at the helm, she was looking down at the detached limb and clutching a hand to her mouth. I yelled over the water, "Jimmy, get a gaff and hook that thing! Kim, bring him close enough, then come around to the stern and pick us up. We have to call the Coast Guard."

Within minutes, we were all back aboard the *Revenge*. I had to physically pick Pescador up and carry him across the gunwale from the swim platform, which was now above water, as the bilge pump did its job. He tried several times to jump back aboard the yacht, before we could get far enough away. Then he went up to the foredeck and sat staring at the yacht, his tail sweeping the deck, as he whimpered like he was pining for a long-lost lover.

Jimmy had the forethought to put the leg in the empty bait box, rather than ruin our catch by putting it in the ice-filled fish box. I climbed quickly to the bridge and reached for the VHF mic.

Kim stopped me. "Do you think that leg has anything to do with the arm you found, Dad?"

I thought about it for a second. The odds of two people being dismembered in the same area and the incidents not being related were pretty slim. Contrary to TV shows, there just weren't all that many murders in the Keys.

"Anyone have a cell signal?" I asked around the bridge.

Everyone checked their cellphones and, one by one, shook their heads. "Kim, go down to my bunk. My sat phone is in the chest, under the bunk. Call Marty and tell him to get his ass out here. We'll wait until he's underway before we call the Coasties."

"We should call them now," Linda said. "We're way out of the sheriff's jurisdiction, even mine."

As Kim hurried down the ladder, I turned to Linda. "Those bodies aren't going anywhere, babe. And whatever happened here happened at least a day ago. Whoever did this is miles away. If this *is* related to the case Marty's working on, we should give him first shot at it. While we're outside the twenty-four-mile Contiguous Zone, all of the Gulf Stream in this area is inside the U.S. Economic Zone. It's not going to hurt anything if Marty's the first on-duty LEO on the scene."

A minute later, Kim was back on the bridge. "He's on his way. Said to call him on channel seventy-two."

Switching the frequency, I keyed the mic. "*MV Gaspar's Revenge*, hailing Marty Phillips."

"Go ahead, *Revenge*," Marty's voice called back.

After I gave him our GPS coordinates, there was a momentary delay as he plugged the numbers in his unit. "I'm less than thirty minutes away."

"Roger that," I replied. "You'll get here long before the cavalry. I'll call it in."

I switched back to channel sixteen, the international hailing and emergency frequency. "*MV Gaspar's Revenge*, calling United States Coast Guard."

The response was immediate. "Coast Guard Station, Key West. Go ahead, *Gaspar's Revenge*."

I reported the two bodies aboard the yacht and the leg floating in the water. Then I asked him to dispatch the nearest Coast Guard vessel to our location and gave him the coordinates.

The voice on the radio asked, "What's the name and home port of the vessel in question, *Gaspar's Revenge*?"

"She's a Pershing 76," I replied. "American-flagged, home port of Miami. The name on the stern is *Obsession*."

# CHAPTER EIGHT

The big sedan slowed as it neared the end of I-95, where the interstate became US-1, in the South Miami suburb of Coral Gables. Dave Parsons followed the directions from the monotone voice of the GPS, as it guided him through an industrial area, to an address with a security fence and guarded gate. "CephaloTech" was printed on a small sign on the front of the guard house, and the roof of the building was just visible above a row of trees.

Buzzing the window down, Parsons slowly approached the gate as a security guard stepped out of the small shack. Inside, Parsons could see a second guard. Both men had their right hands near their weapons. They appeared to be a lot more than the typical rent-a-cops.

Showing his credentials to the guard, he said, "Special Agent Parsons, Army CID, to see Delores Juarez."

Leaning closer, the guard examined Parsons's ID carefully, matching the photo to the man in the car. "Do you have an appointment, Mister Parsons?"

Dave grinned slightly. Most people would address him as Agent Parsons. Warrant officers were addressed as Mister, which told him the young man was probably a former soldier. Noting the chevrons on his collar, he returned the favor. "No, Sergeant. I don't need an appointment."

"No, sir," the guard replied with a knowing grin. "You surely don't. But you'll have to wait here for a minute while I call Miss Juarez and let her know you're here."

It only took a moment on the phone, and the guard returned to Parsons's car. "Go forward two hundred yards, sir. There's a guest parking lot on the left, with a second security gate. Another officer will meet you there to escort you to the lobby, where Miss Juarez will meet you. He'll stay with you while you talk with Miss Juarez, then escort you back here."

"Is his shift just starting or ending?"

"Shift change is at sixteen hundred."

Parsons glanced at his watch as a pair of thick metal pilings in front of the car slowly retracted into the pavement. "Hope he likes overtime," Parsons said as he pulled away from the guardhouse.

He drove straight ahead, under a small canopy of ornamental trees that effectively shielded all but the rooftop of the building from sight. Within the ring of trees, the building looked pretty boring. All chrome and reflective glass. The windows at ground level extended nearly the whole length of the front. Spotting the guard walking toward the gated parking lot, Parsons turned into the entrance and buzzed the window down again.

The guard was tall, quite a bit taller than Parsons's five eleven, with shoulders like a bull moose and arms that stretched the fabric of the short-sleeved uniform shirt he wore. Like the others, his hand was close to his sidearm, which was unbuckled. The guard's head turned, scanning the tree line surrounding the building and the entry driveway before coming to rest on Parsons's car.

Parsons felt as if the guard's eyes could look right through the car with X-ray vision, the way he studied Parsons's car through a pair of wraparound sunglasses.

As if satisfied that Parsons presented no threat, the guard pushed a button on a pedestal just inside the fence and the gate lifted up, allowing Parsons to pull into the parking lot. The giant of a man pointed toward the first parking space on the right and Parsons wheeled into it, shut off the engine, and stepped out of the car.

"Overtime's good for me, Mister Parsons," the guard said as he approached. "I'm Captain Miguel Waldrup, head of security. I assume you're here about the Minniches' disappearance?"

"Why I'm here is classified, Captain."

"Not to me, it's not. Nothing goes on inside these gates that I'm not privy to. The only reason CID would send someone is the CephaloTech sniper suit contract with DoD. We're to exhibit it in just three weeks to the various services' special operations commands. There's nothing in that file you have in your briefcase that I haven't either read, redacted, or personally written myself."

"Seems you're up to speed, then," Parsons said, extending his hand. "Special Agent in Charge, Dave Parsons."

When Waldrup took it, Parsons felt as if his whole hand and wrist had been swallowed by one of the huge catfish he used to catch as a kid, back home in Alabama.

"Pleasure to meet you, Mister Parsons. Follow me, please."

As Waldrup led the way, his head was constantly moving from side to side. Parsons figured a blade of grass couldn't grow a fraction of an inch without it being noticed by the man.

"What rank were you?" Parsons asked.

"Medically retired as a captain, sir. Screaming Eagles. Kuwait."

"Medically retired?"

"One wheel is flesh and bone, the other one's titanium and rubber."

Waldrup took a card from his shirt pocket and held it to a scanner beside the large, reflective tinted-glass door at the main entrance. There was a beep, and a tiny receptacle folded out from the scanner, with a clear brown pad on its surface. Waldrup placed his left thumb on it, and a moment later a dull metallic thud emanated from the door lock.

A cold blast of conditioned air escaped as the door automatically swung inward. Parsons followed Waldrup through the door into a tiny foyer surrounded by more smoked glass, impenetrable to the eye.

The door behind them closed and the lock reengaged. Waldrup looked to the left and nodded, then a second door opened in front of them, revealing a large, high-ceilinged lobby area. Against the far wall was a security desk and yet another security station beside the glass foyer. Both were manned by serious-looking young guards.

Stepping into the lobby, Parsons noted the exterior walls were solid, no windows. The glass front was fake.

"Your security is exceptional, Captain."

"Thank you, sir. I designed the protocols myself and helped with the design of the lobby area. The exterior walls can withstand anything up to a one oh five."

"Impressive. You've been with the company a long time?"

"Hired on just after I got out of the hospital," Waldrup replied. "Part of the company's disabled and veterans' outreach program. That was all before the big breakthrough a few years back. Mister Minnich liked me and learned about my background in Special Forces. When he was awarded the DoD research contract, he asked me how I'd design the security for a new building. Told him I'd build it so ten of me couldn't get in." The big man shrugged slightly. "Mister Minnich made me head of security then and I worked with the architects to build everything. He even paid for my new foot."

To Parsons, it seemed obvious that Waldrup was a devoted company man and thought very highly of his employer. Being that he was a former paratrooper, Parsons had little doubt of the man's determination and self-discipline.

An elevator next to the security desk opened and a woman several years younger than Parsons stepped out. Tall and slender, with dark skin, hair, and eyes, she strode toward Parsons. She was dressed in business attire, gray jacket and slacks, gray pumps. The short heels clicked on the tile floor of the lobby as she approached.

She extended her hand, and Parsons took it, studying her face. In two-inch heels, she was exactly the same height as Parsons, which put her at about five nine. He guessed she couldn't possibly weigh more than one thirty, probably a runner.

A person's facial expressions and handshake always told Parsons a lot more than their words did. Her grip was firm and dry, her face serious, but with a slight upturn at the corners of her mouth. She seemed genuinely pleased to be meeting him.

"Thank you for coming so quickly, Agent Parsons. My name is Delores Juarez, but please call me Lori. I'm afraid that due to the nature of our work, civilian law enforcement may be at a slight disadvantage, which is why I'm so glad you're here. There are things we simply can't divulge, even to civilian police. I'm hoping that once you know the seriousness of what's going on, your office can expedite the search for Mister and Missus Minnich with local authorities and the Coast Guard."

Her voice sounded solid to Parsons, unwavering, self-assured, and clever, with only the slightest bit of a Cuban accent. Probably American-born, raised by Spanish-speaking Cuban immigrants who'd arrived here before America severed relations with the island country. Her eyes were a deep, dark brown, the surface reflecting the low indirect lighting in the lobby, as if that were just the first of many layers of depth.

Parsons noted that she looked directly into his eyes when speaking, blinking normally. His first impression was that she was a very capable and passionate woman. Someone who would throw herself into her work or leisure activity with equal passion. Also a woman who could be deceitful without many people noticing. Right now he felt she was being forthright and open.

Parsons's professional appraisal was interrupted when he suddenly realized she was a strikingly beautiful woman and much closer to his own age than he had first assumed. She tried to disguise her beauty, and nature disguised her age. Her face had that flawless sort of complexion few women possessed, with only the tiniest creases at the corners of her eyes and lips, indicating she was, or had once been, a happy woman, full of vigor and smiling at life.

Lori Juarez led him to a small seating area off to the left. Aside from Waldrup and three of his security staff, there wasn't anyone else in the lobby.

Three comfortable-looking seats were arranged around a low glass table. Lori motioned to the seat facing the foyer and sat down in the one next to it. Waldrup remained standing just beside her, where he could see Parsons's every movement. He'd removed his sunglasses, hanging them in a slot above the pocket flap of his shirt. Waldrup's eyes were surprisingly blue, denoting, along with his name, a mixed heritage.

*Hispanic mother and white father*, Parsons thought. Probably the second son, at least. The father acquiescing to his wife on a Hispanic first name for the younger son.

"Are you the second or third son, Captain Waldrup?"

"I see you did your research, sir."

"Nope," Parsons said. "Never heard of you until you introduced yourself a moment ago."

"Your deductive powers are well developed, Agent Parsons," Lori said. "Miguel is the youngest of three brothers, all of whom are employed by CephaloTech Security."

He smiled slightly in response, taking a small notebook from his jacket pocket and getting right to business. His agents used electronic devices to keep notes, but Parsons still preferred his notepad. He always had several in his briefcase. In his home office, he had five large boxes filled with old notebooks, each one with a date range written on it.

"When did the Minniches leave on their cruise?" Parsons asked

"Last Friday," Lori replied. "There was a lull in our work and Mister Minnich decided to take the yacht to the west coast, to pick up a friend and his wife. The friend is a lobbyist who helped the company secure a government contract for research and development. Their yacht was scheduled to return this morning, and the last communication with Mister Minnich was yesterday morning, when they were anchored at Mooney Harbor in the Marquesas."

"I'm an Alabama boy, Miss Juarez," Parsons said, his slight accent making the word boy sound like *boeh*. "Where is that exactly?"

"About twenty miles west of Key West, sir," Waldrup replied. "Or one hundred forty-five miles southwest of here." Parsons looked up at the big man, who shrugged. "Good spear fishing out there."

"And the yacht can cover the distance from there to here in a single day?"

"With no problem," Waldrup replied. "She has a cruising speed of thirty-five knots and a top speed just over forty-five. Crew of four, working in shifts. All very experienced. They rode out a hurricane at sea two years ago. Hurricane Wilma. Missus Minnich's dog got swept overboard, though."

Parsons made a few notes, then looked up at Lori. "Did Mister Minnich say what time they planned to leave Mooney Harbor?"

Lori looked up at Waldrup, who said, "I was the one who spoke with him, sir. He checks in with me every twelve hours, at oh six and eighteen hundred hours. They were going to get underway with the evening tide, about seventeen hundred."

"And he didn't check in an hour after their planned departure?" Parsons asked, writing another note in his notebook.

"No, sir. And repeated calls to him and the captain went unanswered. I contacted the Monroe County Sheriff's Office twenty minutes later."

"Twenty minutes?"

"Mister Minnich is punctual to a fault, sir. I knew something was wrong at two minutes past the hour. When I couldn't reach him or the boat, I went down to the security offices and we tried to locate the yacht's position using the onboard satellite telemetry. The GPS was disabled and we couldn't locate it."

"Let me guess," Parsons began. "The sheriff's department down there gave you the runaround about being missing for twenty-four hours."

"Bullshit, and I knew it, sir. So I contacted Colonel Brash at the Pentagon. He's our liaison to the Assistant

Secretary of the Army. Minutes later the sheriff himself calls me back. I couldn't give him details on why, but he began a search immediately. A chopper was dispatched out of Key West, flew over the Marquesas, and advised that there was no yacht fitting the description of the *Obsession* anywhere near there. Coast Guard and Navy are already stretched thin down there, but they put some choppers up, too."

Parsons wrote furiously. "How big an area are they searching?"

"At first, only the fifty-mile stretch on the ocean side of Highway One, from the Marquesas to Big Pine Key and out to the Gulf Stream. That's about eight hundred square miles."

"And now?"

"By noon, due to the speed the *Obsession* is capable of, the search was expanded in a circle one hundred nautical miles out from the Marquesas. Over thirty thousand square miles of water."

Parsons stopped writing midsentence. "That's a lot of ocean."

"A drop in a bucket," Lori said. "The *Obsession* has a cruising range of three hundred miles and she'd just taken on fuel in Naples the day before. From the Marquesas, the yacht could travel another two hundred and fifteen miles."

"She could easily make the Bahamas," Waldrup added. "Or Boca Raton, Tampa, or even the western tip of Cuba."

"Cuba?" Parsons asked, looking up at the head of security.

"Our work is something that other countries would like to have," Lori said.

"Which brings us to the why, Miss Juarez."

"General Bottoms apprised me of your security level," she replied. "Follow me, please."

Parsons followed Lori and Waldrup to the elevator. Inside, she swiped a card in front of a sensor and another panel slid out, just like the one by the entry door. She pressed her left thumb on the pad, and it pinged and then retracted. Lori then pressed an unmarked button and the elevator doors silently closed.

The car began to descend. The light for the basement, where Waldrup had said his security offices were located, flashed for a moment. But the elevator didn't stop. It continued down for several more seconds.

"Our lab is twenty-five feet below ground," Waldrup explained. "The floor between the security offices and the lab is five feet of reinforced concrete and steel."

"Quite an achievement in a city barely above sea level."

Waldrup only nodded. When the door opened, Lori stepped out, motioning Parsons to follow. There were rows of electronic equipment, desks, and people bustling around. In the center of the room was a large round pedestal, ten feet across, the surface only a couple of feet above the floor.

Lori stopped in front of the pedestal, Parsons stopping next to her. He looked around the vast room at all the activity. "Very impressive," he said. "And busy."

"We're undergoing the final round of testing right now. The CephaloSuit will be undergoing all kinds of background tests for the next two weeks, to make sure it's ready for anything before the presentation."

"CephaloSuit?" Parsons asked. "What exactly is that?"

Lori turned toward Parsons. "It's the most advanced camouflage suit ever developed. Cephalopods are a group of sea creatures including octopi and cuttlefish. It's the cuttlefish's ability to change color at will that we've been trying to mimic. The wearer will be virtually invisible to the naked eye, as well as thermal imaging. Are you familiar with the ghillie suit used by military reconnaissance teams and snipers?"

"Yes, I was infantry before moving to CID."

"Imagine a ghillie suit that can change color, like a chameleon. So precise in its ability to match any background instantly that even if the background changes abruptly, it will adapt."

She nodded at a man sitting on the other side of the pedestal in front of a small console. Suddenly, the pedestal changed to a black-and-white check pattern, then the pattern began to swirl, resembling a checkered flag flying in the wind. The checks changed colors, first to red and green, then blue and yellow. Lines of assorted colors undulated like psychedelic snakes across the swirling checkerboard.

After a moment the pedestal returned to plain white. "Agent Parsons, would you be kind enough to stare at the center of the table and very quickly move sideways several steps?"

Parsons did as she instructed, moving quickly to his left as he studied the middle of the pedestal. At first, he thought he detected a minute change in the surface, as if it were a bubbling liquid. He assumed it was the hypnotic effect of the multicolored light show.

"Did something appear unusual when you moved?" Lori asked.

He slowly returned to her side, while still watching the surface of the pedestal. "When I moved fast, it appeared as though the surface texture changed a little."

Lori turned toward the pedestal. "Major Roberts?"

Again, Parsons saw swirls emanate from the pedestal, but it wasn't changing color. Something seemed to be moving on top of it, growing higher, until it nearly reached the ceiling. It was like looking through an old glass windowpane, back when glass wasn't made so perfectly flat. The man at the control console on the other side, and the equipment behind him, seemed to waver slightly and shimmer as though Parsons were looking through a prism.

Suddenly, a vision appeared above Parsons's head, like a window to nowhere had opened. A man's face, floating in the air, looked down at him. Parsons blinked his eyes in disbelief.

"Good afternoon, Mister Parsons," the disembodied face said, looking straight at him. "I'm Major Frank Roberts, USMC."

Parsons moved quickly left and right, while looking straight ahead. Making rapid movements, he was able to detect the subtle changes that outlined the man's invisible body, just below his very visible face. It looked as if he could see right through him.

"I'll be damned," Parsons said. "It really is a Predator suit."

# CHAPTER NINE

Marty pulled into Sombrero Resort early. He'd texted the English forensics lady before leaving his apartment, letting her know he'd be out front in ten minutes.

Only one person was outside the lobby, a young woman about twenty-five, with a large black suitcase, whom he'd never seen before, He assumed this was her, but she showed no interest as he pulled in. Her eyes were on the driveway entry, as if waiting for someone.

When he opened the door and got out, the woman glanced at him and smiled, seeing his uniform. She walked toward him, with her hand out. "I was expecting an American police car," she said, Marty recognizing the voice and accent.

"My police vehicle is a boat," he said, taking her hand. "Deputy Marty Philips. I assume you're Meg Stewart?"

"Very nice to meet you, Marty. I'm quite anxious to see your arm and help in any way I might."

Opening the door to his pickup, Marty took her suitcase and put it in the small backseat area of the extended-cab Dodge. It took Meg a moment to figure out which foot to put on the step to get into the raised vehicle. Once she was inside, Marty closed the door and trotted around the hood.

As he climbed in, Meg said, "I still can't get used to your gigantic American cars. Is it far to the morgue?"

"Just a couple of miles. It used to be in the hospital, but the county just built a brand new facility up island."

Minutes later, Marty pulled off the highway onto the crushed coral road to the ME's office on Grassy Key. He parked under a poinciana tree across from the entrance to the building, even though there were a number of empty spots in front of it.

"Reserved parking?" Meg asked.

Marty looked at her, confused, and she pointed to the empty spots in front. "Oh, no," he replied. "Not reserved. Most people around here will park in the shade, even if it's a longer walk."

Climbing out, Marty hurried around the back of the truck, but Meg had already stepped down. She was a pretty woman, a little on the short side, so it was a bit of a descent. Her brown, wavy hair was pulled back in a loose ponytail, hanging past her shoulders.

The sun was barely up, but the overnight temperature never got below eighty, so it was already warm, even for November.

"I can understand why," Meg said, reaching for her suitcase in back. Marty reached for it at the same time, and the two bumped shoulders, turning to look at one another. "Is the weather here always so sultry?"

Picking up her case, Marty said, "It's usually a bit cooler this time of year, but the wind's out of the south. We'll probably get some weather this afternoon."

Inside, Marty introduced Meg to the ME's assistant, a young man named Clyde Barnes. Clyde checked her ID against his list of expected visitors, then rose from the desk.

"Right this way, Marty," Clyde said. Though they were several years apart in age, the two men knew each other, as most people in a small town, on a small island, will.

"You from Australia, Mizz Stewart?" Clyde asked as he led them down the hall to the morgue.

"Britain," she corrected him. "And it's Miss, or just Meg." Marty got the impression she said that for his benefit.

At the door, Clyde punched several buttons on the keypad by the door. It whisked open, cold air carrying the sterile chemical smell into the hallway.

"Just holler on the intercom if you need anything," Clyde said and returned to his desk in front.

Crossing the morgue, Marty was glad there were no bodies lying around. "The arm's right over here, Meg."

Opening the same drawer as yesterday, Marty pulled the cover back so Meg could inspect the arm. Bending over it, she studied the severed end for a moment, then looked around the room.

"Could you pull that tray cart over, Marty?"

He wheeled the cart next to her and placed her case on top of it. Meg opened the case, turning the cart to position it beside her. From a pouch, she removed a small head lamp and pulled it over the top of her head, switching it on and adjusting the beam.

From another pouch, she removed a magnifying glass and a pair of latex gloves. She pulled the gloves on and bent over the arm, holding the glass up in front of her face as she inspected the bone.

Reaching for the small tray the arm lay on, she looked up and asked, "May I turn it round?"

"Please," he replied. "Anything you need."

Turning the tray, she examined the severed end more closely. After a moment, she removed a small digital camera from the case and took several very close-up pictures of the end of the bone.

"This was definitely done with a chain saw," Meg said, not looking up. "Any idea how long it was in the water?"

"Doc Fredric says probably less than twenty-four hours, based on scavenging."

"You have some hungry foragers here," she quipped.

"Water's always warm. Lots of crabs, lobster, and fish."

Putting the magnifying glass and camera aside, she removed a small instrument that looked like a portable TV, along with a pair of hemostats and a very thin cable. She plugged the cable into the TV and switched it on.

Moving her examination further down the arm, to where the muscle and flesh were still attached, she gently moved the gnawed meat this way and that. She finally found what she was looking for and grabbed it with one of the hemostats, ratcheting the clamp-like device onto whatever it was and pulling it out slightly.

"This is the brachial artery, Marty. The main artery in the arm. On the inside of the elbow, it branches into the radial and ulnar arteries. It's at that branch where blood is usually drawn."

Marty watched as she used the second, smaller hemostat and inserted one jaw of it into the blood vessel. Clamping it, she then released the other hemostat and laid it aside.

"Now we may take a look inside the artery," Meg said.

"Are you a doctor?" Marty asked, marveling at Meg's dexterity.

"Not exactly," she replied with a smile as she carefully began to insert the end of the tiny cable into the artery. "I did study at King's College of London, majoring in life science and medicine. But in my fourth year, I discovered I preferred working with dead people, rather than trying to keep the living from becoming one."

She glanced up at him and smiled again. "Does that seem odd to you?"

"Odd?" Marty asked as Meg slowly and carefully moved the cable into the arm, a fraction of an inch at a time, while watching the screen on the little TV. "Nothing odd about trying to help others, even if it means doing unusual things to help solve a crime."

"Here," Meg said. "Come round to this side and have a look."

Stepping around the table, Marty leaned over close to Meg's face in front of the little monitor. "The end of my arterial endoscope is into the ulnar artery now, just past the branch in the elbow."

Marty wasn't sure what he was looking at. It resembled the inside of a pink straw, with the end pinched closed. Meg looked at him, their faces only inches apart.

"I'm, uh, not really sure what I'm supposed to be seeing."

"The artery is collapsed, no clotting of blood," she said, softly. "Your victim was indeed very much alive when this arm was removed."

Marty stood up straight. "What would it look like if he'd been dead?"

"When a person dies," Meg replied, slowly removing the endoscope tube, "the heart stops pumping and the blood will almost immediately begin to coagulate, forming tiny clots that get larger over time. A liver probe is the best way to determine time of death, but a look inside the arteries works as well. If the body isn't moved, livor mortis will set in, blood will pool in the most dependent, or lowest, part, and you'll see what appears to be faint bruising in that area."

"So there's no doubt about it? This man was killed with a chain saw?"

"Perhaps," Meg said, removing the smaller hemostat and placing it with the other. "Without the rest of the body it's impossible to tell. This man may have had this arm cut off and while he was still alive his attacker might have shot him in the head. The bullet would be the cause of death then. Or perhaps he died when another limb was removed and that would be the COD."

"How long could a man live after having his arm hacked off with a McCulloch?"

"McCulloch?"

"It's a popular chain saw manufacturer, here in the States."

"Ah, of course," Meg said. "I thought I'd recognized the name, but this wasn't done with a McCulloch. To answer your question, not very long without medical attention. The brachial artery isn't as large as the femoral artery in the leg, but without medical attention, the victim would die from exsanguination, blood loss, within fifteen minutes or so."

"You can tell what company manufactured the saw that was used?" Marty asked.

"Not in this case, but the kerf marks are not from any American manufacturer, and well over half the chain saws used in the world are manufactured in the United States. I can't say for certain, but the kerf marks resemble one of a number of saws that are manufactured in Eastern Europe."

"What if we find the saw? Any way to match it to the kerf marks?"

"Possibly," Meg replied, wheeling the cart to a sink to clean her instruments. "If the chain has been sharpened, or if it's been well used, there's a very good chance that microscopic tool marks or scratches on either the cutters, the depth gauge, or even the drive links might be matched to marks on the bone. Do you have a saw in evidence?"

"No," Marty replied. "Not yet."

"A positive attitude. I like that."

She turned and began washing off the instruments, then dried them carefully before putting everything away in her case and peeling off the gloves.

"Anything else you can tell me?" Marty asked.

"Yes," Meg replied with a smile. "I'm quite famished. I thought you mentioned breakfast before we were to come here."

"Oh jeez, I'm sorry, Meg. I was just so anxious to get some information." Glancing at his watch, he realized it was already past breakfast, and his own stomach was rumbling. "How about an early lunch?"

"Brunch would be wonderful. Is there a local place that serves good fish? I've heard so much about the fishing here."

"Sure, the *Rusty Anchor* is just before we get back to the resort. Old Rufus is known all over the Keys for his blackened hogfish."

Ten minutes later, they were sitting at the outside bar with several locals, watching Rufus perform. His antics over the grill and stovetops was one of the many reasons people came to the *Rusty Anchor*. His delicious concoctions were all the other reasons.

"Mistah Mahtee," Rufus said as he turned around and noticed the two newcomers to his outdoor kitchen. "What can I and I make for you, mon?"

Marty looked at Meg, and she just shrugged. "I'm quite easy to please. Whatever you recommend."

Rufus smiled at her. "Yuh a long way from home, missy. Chiswick, what I and I be guessin'."

Meg smiled broadly at the old man. "Yes! You have quite an ear, sir."

"Ah, don be callin' old Rufus sahr, missy. I and I are just a cook. Nuting mwore."

"Then please call me Meg, Rufus. I love Jamaican food, and the spicier the better."

"Yuh like di tings dat fly through di air, di ones dat crawls on di groun', crawls on di bottom a Muddah Ocean, or swims?"

"Di ones dat swim in Muddah Ocean, mon," Meg said with a gleeful smile, fully enjoying herself.

Rufus winked at her and turned to Marty. "Jest get some fresh hogfish in, Mistuh Mahtee. Dey was swimmin' just two hours 'go."

"No need to even ask, Rufus," Marty replied.

The old man spun back around to his grills and burners, flipping burgers and chicken with a spatula in one hand and taking pinches of herbs and spices from several bowls with the other, to sprinkle on the meat.

"What a sweet old man," Meg whispered.

"And the best chef in the Keys," Marty replied, leaning closer. "He retired from a five-star restaurant in Jamaica quite a few years back and works part-time here for Rusty now. Some say he's a mystic."

"That would explain his familiarity with regional accents. We Brits travel to Jamaica quite often."

It was past noon when Marty pulled out of the *Anchor* to take Meg back to the resort. As he approached the turn, his cellphone vibrated in his pocket. Pulling it out, he didn't recognize the number, but answered it anyway.

"Marty, it's Kim. We're out on the Stream, and you need to get out here quick. We found a leg!"

# CHAPTER TEN

B y the time the Coast Guard cutter *Key Biscayne* arrived from Key West, Marty had already secured the scene. He'd arrived with a young woman, who he introduced as Meg Stewart, a forensics specialist from England who was working with him on the severed arm case.

With Linda and me helping, we carefully searched the entire yacht. There were no more bodies or body parts to be found. A boat this size would have to have a crew of at least four, I figured, working in shifts if they'd planned any kind of long cruise, and it's not the kind of yacht the owner would pilot himself. Only the dead couple in the forward guest stateroom could be found.

"My guess is the crew members were murdered on the sundeck," Marty told the young Coast Guard lieutenant in command of the *Key Biscayne*. "Their bodies were cut up with a chain saw and thrown overboard."

"Easy speculation," Lieutenant Spears replied. "But what I'd like to know foremost is why a Monroe deputy is first on scene."

"I'm friends with Captain McDermitt," Marty replied.

"And I called him first," I said, playing the dumb charter boat skipper. "I knew he was working a case up in Marathon involving an arm."

"You think this is related?" Spears asked Marty.

"I'd bet on it," Marty replied. "Miss Stewart says the femur has the same kerf marks as an arm that was found up in the Content Keys just yesterday. Both seem to have been made from a chain-saw-wielding assailant. And there are indications that both were done ante mortem."

"Ante mortem?" Lieutenant Spears asked.

"As in before they died," Rusty chimed in.

"You can tell that from the cuts?"

"Not so much the cuts themselves," Meg replied. "Though I am one hundred percent certain both amputations were made with the same saw. The arm I examined this morning was definitely removed while the man was alive and breathing. Judging from the amount of blood on the yacht's sundeck, I feel certain that it happened there while the victim was still alive. If it was done post mortem, there wouldn't be nearly as much blood. Even from four victims, as Captain McDermitt has mentioned would be needed to run this yacht."

Spears visibly shuddered. "Son of a bitch," he muttered.

"I have a towboat on the way, Lieutenant," Marty said. "But, since we're outside U.S. territorial waters, and both Agent Rosales and I are well beyond our legal jurisdictions, I need your permission to move the yacht to the Marathon City Marina, where our crime scene investigators can gather evidence."

"I'll grant permission, once I get the okay from my superiors. Shouldn't be a problem, since Marathon is much closer. But I know I'll be ordered to escort the yacht in."

"Why?" Linda asked. "The Coast Guard doesn't usually investigate murders."

"We've been searching for this yacht since Thursday evening, Agent Rosales. The owner is a military contractor." Turning back to Marty, he added, "Don't be surprised if one or more alphabet agencies isn't waiting at the dock to take over your investigation, Deputy. I'll let you know what my superiors say."

With that, the lieutenant and two petty officers boarded their tender to head back over to the cutter.

"Guess there's nothing left to do here but wait for Sea Tow," Rusty said.

We'd left the *Obsession* adrift and moved away from the yacht after the search so it was downwind. It'd been a couple of hours since we'd found her, and whatever Rufus had put in that little bottle had worn off after exactly one hour. Using it a second time did nothing.

"Y'all don't need to hang around," Marty said. "The towboat'll be here in about ten minutes."

"Hell, we come this far," Rusty said. "There's plenty of ice on the fish we caught and I'm curious what all this government stuff's about. I vote we hang around."

"I know how we might be able to get a little more information," Linda offered.

"Chyrel!" Kim said. "If she can't dig something up, there's nothing buried."

"Okay," I said. "Let's all go in the salon and see if she can come up with anything."

"If it's alright with you, Jesse," Marty said, "I need to keep the crime scene in visual contact. Mind if I sit on your bridge?"

I whisked my hand toward the ladder. "Be my guest. I can open the intercom and you can hear anything Chyrel digs up."

"I'll keep you company," Kim said as she started up the ladder.

"Care to join us inside, Miss Stewart?" I asked. I'd seen the way Kim had bristled when Marty pulled up with the English woman on his patrol boat. "You can't ask who it is we're going to talk to, though."

In the salon, I booted up the laptop and clicked on the "Soft Jazz" icon. This actually opens a direct video feed to Chyrel Koshinski's office in Homestead. Or wherever she has one of her computers turned on. I don't know how the hardware works with satellites, but it does. She's one of Deuce's team members, and a former CIA computer analyst who could hack into any computer system devised by man or machine.

After a minute, a window opened to a plain white background and the corner of a desk. It jiggled and turned away from the corner, then Chyrel stepped into the screen and sat down.

"Hey, Jesse. Been a while. Sorry for the delay. I had to set up my laptop. The PC went down just as you called. What's up with you?"

"Hi, Chyrel," I said. The woman was always bubbly and upbeat, enthusiastic about life itself. "Your PC went down? Why am I having trouble with that?"

"Shit happens," she said with a grin, her short blond hair pulled back in a sloppy ponytail. "I don't build 'em, I just make 'em do more than they were designed to."

"Hey, look, we're out here on the Gulf Stream and came across an abandoned vessel."

"We?"

"Yeah, I brought Linda, Jimmy, Rusty, and Kim out fishing."

"So, you're halfway to Cuba and find a derelict boat. Not real unusual in that area, is it?"

"This one is, Chyrel. It's a large luxury yacht with a dead couple on board. The Coasties are just off our starboard side, waiting for a towboat. I was hoping you might be able to shed some light on who owns the boat."

Interlocking her fingers, she extended her hands palm out, cracking her knuckles. "What's the name of the boat?"

"*Obsession*, out of Miami," I replied. "It's a seventy—"

"A seventy-six-foot Pershing," Chyrel said, interrupting me. "Owned by Darius Minnich and his wife Celia, the CEO and CFO of a company called CephaloTech in Coral Gables."

Raising my eyebrows, I leaned toward the computer in disbelief. "You're fast, Chyrel, but not that fast. How'd you know it already?"

"Are you kidding? Every agency from the Miami dogcatcher to the CIA has been looking for it for almost two days. CephaloTech is working on a top secret project for DoD."

"You hear that, Marty?" I said in the direction of the intercom. "Your case has national security implications."

His voice came back over the speaker. "Yeah, I heard. Now they're gonna yank it."

"Chyrel," I said, turning back to the laptop, "Marty's working on a murder case involving a severed arm I found up near my island. From the looks of things, that arm might have been one of the *Obsession* crew members."

"Yikes!" she said. "What is it with people down there?"

"Hey, it's not us," I said with a grin. "Outsiders. We go by the live-and-let-live rule."

"So, what is it you want me to find out next?"

I thought for a moment. "Coast Guard's already called it in. By now, I'm sure word is out to all the interested parties. Can you find out who's gonna take the case from Marty? And if the dead couple are the owners?"

"That's easy," she replied. "I learned about the disappearance of the boat and its owners while surfing JDISS, the Joint Deployable Intelligence Support System. Something I do when I'm bored. I already have a little bit of information. Apparently, this CephaloTech outfit is working on a really sensitive, high-tech camouflage system, under a DoD contract awarded by the Assistant Secretary for Army Acquisitions, an Air Force general by the name of Clyde Bottoms. So, Marty, your first guest will most likely be Army CID. The usual turf war will be waged between them, FBI, CIA, and probably a few more."

"Damn," I heard Marty mutter through the intercom.

"But, then again," Chyrel said with a grin, "the whole alphabet soup falls under the oversight of one agency. Not the Army, though. Want me to see if I can pull some strings?"

Turning to Rusty, I said, "There's something I wasn't supposed to tell you, bro. But if this conversation goes another minute, you're likely to find out. Stockwell's taking his old job back."

Rusty stood up. "What the? What about Deuce? I thought he was doing great up there."

"Long story," I replied. "I'll tell ya more about it later. But Deuce and Julie will be home tomorrow afternoon. Act startled, okay? For your daughter's sake? She wants to surprise you."

The grin on my old friend's face grew wider with each passing second. He hadn't seen his only living relative, his daughter Julie, in several months now, and the two had been inseparable since the day she was born. "Yeah, sure, I'll play along."

Turning back to the laptop, I said, "Tell Travis that I'd consider it a personal favor if Marty can at least remain on the case in some capacity."

"Will do, but he's gonna want quid pro quo," Chyrel replied with a grin of her own.

"The Cay Sal Bank?"

"You can almost bet on it," Chyrel replied with a wink.

"Well, don't offer it to him. But can you fax me everything you have on it, without anyone knowing?"

"Oh, please."

"Okay," I said with a chuckle. "Send me what you can, before you ask him. Then I can decide if the kid's worth me sticking my neck out for."

"You got it, Jesse," Chyrel said. Two photos appeared side by side on the screen. A man in his late fifties probably, with salt-and-pepper hair and a wide face. The other picture was a younger woman, very attractive, with piles of blond hair past her shoulders.

"Is this the dead couple?" Chyrel asked.

"Definitely not the woman," I replied. "And the dead man is only slightly gray around the temples, maybe ten years younger than what the guy in the picture looks to be."

"Probably guests of the owners," Chyrel said.

Marty's voice came over the speaker. "That means either the owners are dead and fed to the fish, or they've been kidnapped."

"Thanks, Chyrel," I said. "Let me know what Travis says."

"I'll call Linda," Chyrel said, grinning. "Your phone's probably in the freezer or somewhere like that. Bye, y'all."

The window closed and the desktop screen returned. I closed the laptop and looked around the salon. "Grab a cooler and some drinks, will ya, Jimmy? Let's go up to the bridge."

# CHAPTER ELEVEN

Parson's was at the CephaloTech gate the next morning at nine. His interview Friday evening with Miss Juarez and Captain Waldrup lasted several hours, and he came away from it convinced that neither was involved and fairly certain it had nothing to do with anyone in the company, since the two of them were the only ones that had known the missing couple's travel plans. Today, he planned to dig into the background of anyone else close to the couple.

Two military policemen were there waiting by the rear bumper of a white Chevy sedan, parked to the right of the gate. Both were dressed in casual civilian clothes and sport jackets. Approaching the gate, Parsons buzzed the window down, and the same guard as the day before stepped out of the shack.

"Your men have been here for a few minutes, Mister Parsons," the guard said. "I told them they'd have to wait here. They'll need to ride in with you, sir. Captain Waldrup doesn't like a lot of vehicles in the inner lot."

Parsons stepped out of the car and walked around the back, motioning the two MPs toward him. As they approached, he held out his ID and said, "Special Agent in Charge, Dave Parsons. You two will accompany me in my car."

"Pleased to meet you, Mister Parsons," the shorter of the two said, a black man about thirty years old. "I've heard a lot about you, sir. I'm Staff Sergeant Barry Pitts and this is Sergeant Terence Brahm." The taller sergeant carried a computer case over his shoulder.

"Call me Dave, alright? I'll be a civilian in a few weeks."

The three men shook hands and got into Parsons's car. As the guard lowered the barricade posts in front of the car, Parsons flipped through his notepad. Finding the page he wanted, he handed it to the sergeant in the backseat. "See what you can dig up on this couple, Terence. The man's a lobbyist who worked on getting funding for CephaloTech research."

"What kind of research are they doing?" Barry asked.

"I assume you both have a top secret clearance?"

"Yes, sir, we do," Barry replied.

"CephaloTech is working on a new high-tech ghillie suit. I saw a small demonstration of it yesterday. Thing's amazing. It'll allow our recon and sniper guys to just sit right down in an enemy camp if they want to, and never be seen." Glancing over his shoulder at the man in the backseat, he added, "The couple was with the head of CephaloTech and his wife two days ago, when the yacht they were on disappeared. I wanna know if either the lobbyist or his wife have any ties to Cuba, or any other country or entity that might want to steal the technology."

Turning into the entry for the parking area, Waldrup was already waiting. He raised the gate, still looking around the perimeter as he had the previous day. This morning, Waldrup looked a bit haggard, though. Parsons parked the car and the three soldiers got out. He introduced Waldrup to the two men.

"Any updates?" Parsons asked Waldrup.

"No, sir. I spent the night in the security office, following up on the search. Most of my men did the same thing. We have a bunk area in case of emergency."

"Sergeant Brahm here is looking into the backgrounds of the lobbyist and his wife. Anything you can tell him?"

"Mister Proctor is just what he seems," Waldrup began as they approached the front door to the building. "A career lobbyist with a fat wallet. His only concern is moving money from one hand to another, skimming part of it off the top."

"I take it you're not a fan of the financial process used in Congress?"

"Not a bit, sir," Waldrup replied, swiping his card and thumbing the console. "At least not on the outside. Money is needed for research, I get that. But burying the request in a completely unrelated bill is just stupid. Our research here is vital, as you now know. Such funding should be supplied based on the merit of the research. Instead, we have to use lobbyists to compete for dollars that might go to researching gay Tibetan monkeys."

The outer door whisked inward and the three men entered, Waldrup nodding to the guard on the other side of the one-way glass.

"What about his wife? Know anything about her?"

"She's my mother's cousin," Waldrup replied as the inner door opened and the four men headed to the corner where Lori Juarez was already waiting, a laptop open in front of her.

"So, your opinion of her might be biased?" Parsons asked. "Sorry, but in my experience, relatives make the worst character references."

"In most cases, I'd agree with that, Mister Parsons," Waldrup replied, seeming to take no offense. "In the case of Eliana, though, trust me, she's no different than her husband in most ways. He's rich and middle-aged. She's a gold digger, young and beautiful. They were made for each other. If it weren't for her looks, she'd be working in a liquor store in Opa-Locka." Tapping a finger to his temple, he added, "Not much upstairs, but she has a great staircase."

Lori rose from her seat as the men approached. Though she wore a skirt today, it was simple business attire, as understated as the previous day. Parsons introduce her to the two MPs.

Lori sat down on the edge of her seat, crossing her legs and tucking them to the side. *Probably a habit born of her desire to be inconspicuous*, Parsons thought. To be accepted for her mind and not her looks.

Parsons took the same seat as before, with his back to the wall, and Barry motioned to Terence to take the remaining seat so he could work on his computer on the table.

"Do you think either Jacob or Eliana Albright might have told anyone where they were going?" Parsons asked Waldrup, referring to the lobbyist and his wife.

"Only that they were going to Miami," the captain replied. "It was Missus Minnich's idea to stop in the Marquesas. She and Eliana both like to swim and snorkel. Mister Minnich is more into wreck diving. Same with Mister Albright. Mooney Harbor is pretty big and shallow. Great for snorkeling and looking at tropical fish."

"I doubt you'll find anything on the Albrights," Lori said. "He works on all kinds of funding requests, from environmental concerns to weapons manufacturing."

"For money," Parsons said. *Always follow the money* was Parsons's primary goal in any investigation. Nearly every crime had some basis in monetary gain. "Pretty good money from the sound of it," he added.

"Yes, but these types of people have to be squeaky clean," Lori said. "Otherwise, they couldn't be trusted by either party they negotiate with."

"True," Parsons said, taking out his notebook. "But, if offered that one big score?"

"I suppose anyone could be tempted," Lori said, the corners of her mouth turning up ever so slightly.

"I contacted the Pentagon last night," Parsons said. "Just to give an update on what was going on. I was assured more assets would be diverted to the search. Where are we this morning?"

"I'm actually following the search in real time," Lori said. "General Bottoms arranged access for me. Right now there are two helicopters each from the Navy, Coast Guard, and Monroe Sheriff's office up in the air, working a three-hundred-and-sixty-degree grid search, plus

a Coast Guard cutter from Key West and other smaller boats from Marathon and Islamorada are searching.
Nothing reported so far."

Parsons asked questions and jotted down notes as
Terence Brahm continued digging into the background
on the Albrights. Pitts and Waldrup stood off to the side,
having found a common link in the infantry. At noon,
Lori suggested they move upstairs to the cafeteria, where
they could talk and have lunch at the same time.

In the elevator, standing next to Miss Juarez, Parsons detected the faintest scent of perfume, something
he hadn't noticed the previous day.

All five of them sat down at a large round table, an
actual waiter waiting to take their lunch orders. "Please,
order whatever you like," Lori said, motioning Parsons
to the seat next to her. "Our kitchen staff is equal to any
restaurant."

Glancing over the menu, Parsons ordered a cheese-
burger and fries, then continued asking questions, now
turning to the Minniches' background, particularly Mister Minnich's first wife, Darlene.

"From what he's told me," Lori said, "Mister Minnich
has had zero contact with her since their divorce. They'd
been married twelve years, no kids. She didn't want any,
but he did and thought he could change her mind. I'm
not even sure if she's still living in the area."

"Bad divorce? Equitable split?"

"From what I gather, it was less than equitable at
the time. Mister Minnich was taken by surprise when
she left. He was down in the dumps for weeks. He didn't
even hire a lawyer, I don't believe. Darlene hired a good

attorney and received most of the marital assets and alimony."

"Since then?" Parsons asked.

Lori thought a moment. "Well, there was the one time," she finally said. Parsons leaned forward. "Her lawyer didn't go far enough. I guess Darlene never expected Mister Minnich to succeed the way he has. Her alimony wasn't increased when CephaloTech received the Department of Defense contract. I guess he did sort of reach out to her after the contract was awarded. When he came out of his stupor, he began seeing Celia. She worked in the lab then. Mister Minnich sent Darlene an invitation to their wedding. It was on a private island in the Eastern Caribbean."

Parsons considered it. Money was a big player in this case, had to be. He was now convinced that the Minniches had been kidnapped. CephaloTech was on the verge of selling billions of dollars' worth of technology to the military and could probably equal that in sales to our allies. A kidnapper could demand a very high ransom. His thumbing his nose toward his ex-wife in that way had been sophomoric at best. But damned if Parsons didn't like the guy's style.

Just then, Lori's phone, which was sitting next to her laptop, began to buzz. As she reached for it, Parson's own phone vibrated in his pocket. As she answered hers, he saw that he had a text message from Colonel Brash's aide. It was only five words.

*Obsession found. Proceed to Marathon.*

# CHAPTER TWELVE

After the threat of the chain saw was removed, Darius told the man that he would give them anything, tell them anything, if they'd not hurt his wife. He wasn't sure how long ago that had been. The two men had left without a word. He'd talked to his wife then, trying to reassure her. The very real threat of being hacked up with a chain saw frightened her a great deal.

The thought of watching it done to the woman he loved, having suddenly and completely recalled the spectacle on the sundeck as his captain and crew were literally executed one limb at a time, scared him enough that he'd do or say anything.

If he turned over the information they wanted and their captors released him and Celia, they'd probably have to flee the country. Patriots are supposed to give their lives rather than divulge secrets.

Darius would do that without hesitation, if it were only himself. He loved his country. If they killed his wife, they'd get nothing and would have to execute him as well. But, cut off one of her arms and sell her as a one-armed sex slave? Darius would do anything.

The husband and wife had talked after the men left. They'd tried escaping their bonds, but it was hopeless. The timbers they were tied to were strong and thick, and their restraints were large nylon zip ties, so tight they bit into the flesh of their wrists, their upper arms, and Celia's bare ankles.

Once their captors got the information they wanted, there was a very real chance they would be killed anyway. But Darius had one bargaining chip the captors didn't know about, something he might be able to use. It was a long shot, and they'd have to live out their days in a foreign country, but it was probably the only chance they'd have to survive this ordeal and Darius knew it.

He'd explained it to Celia, and they'd discussed the merits, and the likelihood that their captors would go for it, for over an hour. At first, Celia had been against the idea, convinced that these men would release them once they got what they wanted.

Darius knew better. In giving these men the information they wanted, they'd be committing treason. The fact that their lives were at stake would have little or no bearing. His company would be ruined, he and Celia most likely dead and a black mark left on their names.

Finally, exhaustion had overtaken them both, when the men hadn't returned after a couple of hours. The inside of the building had grown very hot, the air heavy with moisture, and both Darius and Celia had passed out.

Darius didn't know how long they'd been asleep when the same two men entered again, the slamming door waking him. The one called Oleg carried a small folding table and chair, with a satchel over his shoulder. *At least he doesn't have the chain saw*, Darius thought.

The leader of the two stood in the near-total darkness, staring at Celia, still passed out. Oleg hung a small battery-operated lantern from a roof beam, then set the table and chair up in front of Darius.

"Ready, Ilya," Oleg said.

The leader turned around. "Go get your tools, Oleg."

When Oleg left, the man called Ilya walked toward Darius, his hands clasped behind his back. "Forgive me for not introducing myself earlier, Mister Minnich. I am Ilya Dobrovska."

"I would say it's a pleasure, Mister Dobrovska," Darius said. "But that would be a lie."

"I too value honesty," Ilya said. "And I will be very honest with you now. I have a client who is going to pay me quite well for the information you are going to provide. I will get that information any way I have to."

Oleg came back through the door then, and Darius could see that he was once more carrying the chain saw. Placing it on the floor in front of Celia, he removed a large pair of pruning shears from his pocket and moved around behind Darius.

Ilya took a small semiautomatic handgun from under his shirt and pointed it in Celia's direction. "Oleg is going to free you now, Mister Minnich. If you move in any way I do not like, I will shoot your wife and then you. I will not kill either of you, I will only shoot to inflict pain. A kneecap, perhaps. Then Oleg will work on your pretty wife with his saw while you watch. Am I making myself perfectly clear to you?"

"Yes," Darius replied with a nod. "I'll cooperate completely."

Ilya nodded his head and Darius felt the tension from the nylon strap on his left wrist tighten for a moment before it fell free, cut by the large pruning shears. One by one, Oleg cut through his restraints.

Free once more, Darius stood with his arms stretched out, as if he were still secured to the beams. He didn't want to do anything to provoke the man.

"You may lower your hands, Mister Minnich."

Slowly, Darius lowered his arms, while he looked straight at the Russian black marketer in front of him.

"We don't have to do it this way," Darius said. "Yes, I know what you're after, and I will give it to you. Freely. After that, if you should kill us, you'll never know of any other discoveries my company has made. Other information that we can also sell to the highest bidder. I wish to be your partner."

# CHAPTER THIRTEEN

I t was late evening before we made our way into Boot Key Harbor. As predicted, the cutter *Key Biscayne* was ordered to escort the towboat and yacht, and we were instructed to accompany them to City Marina, where an agent with the Bureau would have some questions.

Rusty and Jimmy tied off as I stepped over the gunwale and up to the pier with Kim. Before towing the yacht, two Coast Guardsmen in hazmat suits had boarded it and opened all the exterior hatches in an attempt to dissipate the stench of death. It helped. A little. We walked as wide past it as possible.

The sheriff's office had two cruisers at the end of the dock, with crime scene tape blocking anyone from entering the dock area. As we strode toward them, several suits started our way, along with a man in some kind of uniform. The uniformed man towered over the others with shoulders like a professional football player.

"Are you Jesse McDermitt?" one of the men asked. He was close to my age. His hair was cut in a military fashion, but the bushy mustache said otherwise. Two other men were obviously military or cops. The fourth man I recognized as the FBI agent who had helped in the search and failed rescue of my late wife two years earlier.

I extended my hand to the Bureau man. "Binkowski, right?"

He took my hand firmly. "Yes, sir. This is Special Agent in Charge Dave Parsons, with Army Criminal Investigation." Binkowski then nodded to the other two suits and the huge man in a security guard uniform, adding, "Sergeants Pitts and Brahm, Army MPs, and Captain Miguel Waldrup, head of security for CephaloTech. Mister Parsons was in charge of the investigation, until just a moment ago, when we all received orders from DHS."

I looked at the CID man, Parsons. Up close, I could see that he was probably a few years older than me, which meant he was nearing mandatory retirement age.

"So, who's in charge now, Mister Parsons?" I asked, shaking his hand, as Marty and Linda joined us, Linda talking on her cellphone.

"You are, Agent McDermitt," Parsons said.

Linda extended the phone to me. "It's Chyrel. She has Director Stockwell on hold for you."

"Will you excuse me?" I said to the four men, taking Linda's phone and retreating down the dock a way.

Putting the phone to my ear, I said, "Chyrel, what the hell's going on here?"

"Good afternoon, Jesse," a familiar voice said.

"Travis? Is this your doing?"

"Just until Deuce arrives. He and Julie just took off over an hour ago and will land in Marathon just after sunset."

"What the hell did you tell these guys, man? There's an FBI agent, a warrant officer from CID, two MPs, and a gorilla in a security guard's uniform here telling me that I'm in charge."

"You are in charge, Jesse," Associate Deputy Director Travis Stockwell replied. "Deuce will relieve you. You said you wanted to have your deputy friend involved, so involve him."

"I don't know anything about investigating a damned double murder, Colonel."

"You don't have to," Stockwell replied. "Just direct the ones that do. I've put you on the clock. Starting time was when you radioed the Coast Guard. Your usual fee."

"This is totally different, Travis," I whispered angrily. "Screw the money. A couple's lives are at stake here."

"The coroner should arrive soon, along with forensics people. Until then, the yacht is a federal crime scene. You can allow the two agents access, to look. But nobody touches anything until the forensics people get there."

"You're an asshole," I said.

"Yep, earned that title a long time ago, when some general pinned those little birds on my collar. Look, this really is something the CCC should be the lead on, and right now, that's you. When Deuce gets there, he'll take over. Later, you and he can sit down and talk about Cay Sal."

"You got the wrong guy for this," I said. But there was no sound from the phone. Looking at the screen, I saw that the call had been ended. "Son of a bitch," I muttered as I stomped my way back to the group, everyone waiting for me to tell them what to do.

I looked at Marty first. With an FBI agent, an Army CID guy, Linda with FDLE, and two MPs all waiting to investigate the murder of two people on board the yacht, probably four more murdered and fed to the sharks, and two more kidnapped, what does the federal government do? In their infinite wisdom, they put a fisherman and junior sheriff's deputy in charge. No wonder they call it the Puzzle Palace.

"Deputy Phillips," I said, trying to sound professional for his sake. "Find out how long before the coroner and your CSIs get here. You're in charge of securing the scene. Agents Parsons and Binkowski, until I'm told differently, and I haven't been ordered otherwise yet, this is Deputy Phillips's case. He's been working it since yesterday morning when the first clue was found and was assigned the case by order of the top law enforcement person on these islands, the Monroe County Sheriff."

"At the moment," Binkowski said, "you're the top law enforcement person."

"How long have you been down here?" I asked him, beginning to get irritated.

"Two years," Binkowski replied.

"And in that two years, you've never read the Florida constitution? It specifically gives each elected sheriff complete jurisdiction within their counties. Over FDLE, the state police, the FBI, and even DHS. The sheriff assigned this case to Deputy Phillips, and only the sheriff can authorize a federal agency to take it over. Until then, I'm offering the full cooperation of Homeland Security and its subordinate agencies to this deputy. Is that clear?"

"Yes, sir," Binkowski replied, somewhat pissed.

"You don't look like any kind of federal agent to me," the huge security guard said.

Stepping past the four suits, I looked Waldrup squarely in the eye. "I work with the Caribbean Counterterrorism Command, an undercover badged agency of Homeland Security. It's the top-tier federal agency that the FBI, CIA, CID, DEA, and any other letters you can think of that pertain to any federal investigative and law enforcement agency answer to, Captain. If I looked like you, I wouldn't be very effective, would I?"

"Sorry, sir," the human mountain said. "I meant no disrespect. It's just that, well, the dead woman on board might be my cousin."

"There were two couples and four crewmembers on board," Parsons offered. "The report from the Coast Guard said only two bodies were found."

I glared at Parsons. "Two bodies, and an arm and leg from at least one other victim. Deputy Phillips found the arm yesterday, and the leg was in the water by the yacht when it was found."

Marty returned from his patrol boat. "Captain Hammonds said our CSI team should be here any second, and he and the coroner will be here in five minutes."

"Until Hammonds gets here," I said, "you're the top law enforcement officer on the scene, Marty."

Turning to Waldrup, I said, "Sorry, son. If you'll accompany the deputy, perhaps you can identify whose bodies are still aboard."

He started to turn and follow Marty. I put a hand on his bulging shoulder. "It's not very pretty in there."

"Army Airborne, sir. I've seen 'not pretty' before."

I nodded, and he and Marty went aboard the yacht. Turning to the two agents, I asked, "Which of you is most up on the Minniches' disappearance?"

"That'll be me, Agent McDermitt," Parsons said, flipping open a notebook. "I've been interviewing co-workers of the missing couple since yesterday."

"Just Jesse," I said. "What have you come up with?"

"Then call me Dave," he replied, then read from his notebook. "Darius and Celia Minnich left Miami a week ago to cruise to the west coast and pick up another couple, friends and supporters of their work, Jacob and Eliana Albright. They refueled in Fort Myers two days ago before heading south. Their last known location was in the Marquesas, yesterday morning. They planned to depart there at seventeen hundred hours, but failed to check in with Captain Waldrup at their prearranged time an hour after that. Onboard electronics appear to have been turned off, so their location couldn't be determined."

Looking south, out over the harbor, I thought for a moment. "Mooney Harbor has shallow approaches," I said, thinking out loud. "High tide yesterday was about seventeen hundred. It's a good eighty miles from there to where we found the yacht adrift."

"What's that tell you, Jesse?" Linda asked, snapping me from my thoughts.

"I'm sorry," I said. "Dave, Agent Binkowski, this is my girlfriend, Agent Linda Rosales, Florida Department of Law Enforcement, and my daughter Kim."

They all shook hands as I continued my train of thought. "The yacht probably draws too much water to get out of Mooney at any other time. If they left on the high tide at seventeen hundred and didn't check in or couldn't be located at eighteen hundred, that's got to be the time frame the yacht was rigged to sink."

"Sink?" Binkowski asked.

"Yeah, someone deliberately pulled the hose off the bilge pump to sink her. A boat like this couldn't go much faster than forty knots, I'd guess."

"Forty-five," Parsons interjected. "As reported by Captain Waldrup, who seems to know the boat intimately."

"Forty-five knots would put them somewhere in the vicinity of Big Pine an hour after leaving the Marquesas. That'd explain the arm up in the Contents. The current would carry it east and the tide took it north, probably through Spanish Harbor, up to my island."

"Where's that?" Parsons asked.

"Twenty miles northwest of here."

"Currents could carry an arm that far?" Binkowski asked.

"Only if it was tossed overboard in the right place and it was semi-buoyant," I said. "Based on currents and tide, about ten miles west of where we found the yacht adrift in the Gulf Stream. The tidal current through the back country up there is pretty fast." I pointed toward the south-southwest, across the harbor where the mouth of Sister Creek feeds out into the ocean. "About eleven miles that way was where it occurred."

Marty and Waldrup stepped back down to the dock and walked toward us. The security captain wore wrap-around sunglasses like most watermen do around here, his eyes inscrutable behind them.

Marty nodded his head toward the bigger man. "Captain Waldrup has positively identified the bodies as his cousin, Eliana Albright, and her husband Jacob Albright. Evidence suggests sexual assault and execution-style murders."

"No sign of the Minniches?" Binkowski asked.

I knew where he was headed. Kidnapping is the bailiwick of the Bureau. He was jumping the gun by a long shot. There was something more important at the moment.

"Until a ransom demand is made," I said in a low, even tone, "we're going on the assumption that they're missing. Is that clear, Binkowski?"

"Now just wait a minute, McDermitt," Binkowski said. "This has all the earmarks of a kidnapping. And—"

"Shut the fuck up!" I froze him in place with a hard cold stare.

Slowly, I turned to Waldrup. He stood ramrod straight, arms clasped behind his back, eyes a mystery behind his sunglasses.

"*Mi más sentido pésame a su pérdida, Capitán.*"

Nodding, Waldrup said, "Thank you, sir. She didn't deserve to die like that."

"No," I said, feeling my eyes well up slightly. "She didn't."

I jerked my head toward the far end of the dock and started walking, Waldrup falling in step beside me. Changing the subject, I looked out over the water and asked, "You were Airborne?"

"Yes, sir. Seventy-fifth, in Kuwait."

"Then stop calling me sir, dammit. I'm a retired Marine Gunny."

He turned toward me then and removed his shades. His eyes were blue, which I hadn't expected. They were also moist and bloodshot, the latter of which I was pretty sure was because he was tired and overworked. I could sense it in the way he moved and carried himself.

"You lost people?" he asked.

Looking into his eyes, I could see that behind the pain of loss, there was a fire still there. "Yeah, a few," I replied. Then without knowing why, I added, "Someone closer than a cousin was taken in the same way. I really am sorry, soldier."

"You'll help me find out who did this, Gunny? Give me ten minutes alone with them?"

I realized that I was already committed. Stockwell and the Cay Sal Bank would have to wait. "Yeah, we'll find out who did it. You have my word on that. And if it was up to me, I'd give you fifteen minutes."

"Jesse!" Marty shouted. I turned and he pointed to a white van pulling up to the two cruisers at the foot of the pier. "CSI team's here."

"Come on," I said to Waldrup and we marched back to the others.

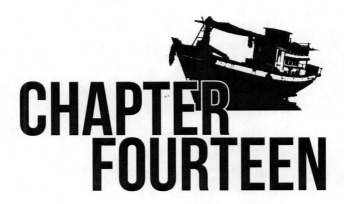

# CHAPTER FOURTEEN

The sheriff's CSI team consisted of two men, both looked to be in their mid- to late forties. Marty introduced them as Lieutenant Richardson and Sergeant Jimenez. The two men wasted no time, going straight aboard the *Obsession*, each carrying two large satchels.

A moment later, the coroner's van pulled in, parking next to the CSI van. Doc Fredric got out of the passenger side and started our way. A younger man got out of the driver's seat and went to the back of the van.

Doc nodded at me and Binkowski, who I guess he'd met before. Then he smiled at Linda, extending his hand. "Agent Rosales, so nice to see you again. Is this your case?"

Linda smiled and shook his hand. "No, actually, it's Jesse's case, and he's put Marty in charge for now."

Doc Fredric looked puzzled for just a moment, then smiled up at me. "So those rumors are true, then."

"I don't know, Doc. I never put much stock in sea stories myself." I introduced him to the others.

"Army CID?" Doc asked, when I introduced Dave Parsons. "How's this connected to the Army? Or should I not ask?"

"I'll tell you what I can, Doctor Fredric. But the reason the Army's interested is classified."

"We don't stand on formality down here, son. How about Doc? That's what everyone else calls me."

"Okay, Doc, and you can call me Dave. That's what everyone will be calling me in a few weeks when I retire. What I can tell you is that Mister Minniches' company, which Captain Waldrup works for, has a research contract with the military. They're scheduled to exhibit a project very soon that they've been working on for several years. It's a vitally important project to the Army. I was assigned by one of the Assistant Secretaries of the Army and report directly to the Pentagon. That's really all I can say right now."

"Jesse!" Jimmy shouted from the cockpit. "Your laptop just started playing Coltrane."

Suddenly, Pescador vaulted over the gunwale and went charging for the yacht, barking at a high nervous pitch. His actions all day had been way beyond normal. I quickly moved into his line of sight and yelled, "Pescador! No!"

As if seeing me for the first time, he stopped and sat down, looking from me to the yacht, whining. "Sorry," Jimmy said, running up behind Pescador. "He's been wanting to get off the boat, since we tied up. Thought he had to piss, man."

Grabbing Pescador's collar, Jimmy tugged on it, calling his name. The dog didn't budge, but jerked his head back, trying to pull out of the collar.

"Pescador!" I said firmly. He instantly sat back down, and I knelt in front of him. Taking his big shaggy head in both hands, I gave him an affectionate shake. "What is it, boy?"

Pescador looked at me as if begging for something. Glancing over to the yacht, he whined again. "Damn, I wish you could talk. Hey! Look at me." When he turned back to me, I said, "Go with Jimmy. Get back on the boat and stay there."

As I stood, Jimmy gave him a gentle tug. Pescador turned and walked back toward the *Revenge* with him, occasionally looking back at the big yacht and whining.

Waldrup had pulled Parsons aside, speaking urgently in a low tone, as I rejoined the group. "Sorry, my dog's never acted like this before. I have no idea what's gotten into him."

"Would you say he might have recognized the yacht?" Parsons asked. "Like he'd seen it before?"

"Yeah," I replied. "That's exactly how I'd describe it."

Waldrup whispered something else to Parsons.

"Deputy Phillips," Parsons said, turning to Marty. "Will you go aboard, please? Go to the master stateroom and bring us the framed photograph mounted on the wall next to the hanging closet door."

Doc's assistant arrived with a single gurney, a large black case on it. "Want me to go ahead and get the second gurney, Doc?"

"Not just yet, Clyde," Doc replied and then turned to me. "With your permission, Jesse, I'd like to go aboard and have a look at the bodies. Have they been identified?"

"Yeah, Doc. Captain Waldrup here is related to the woman, and the man is her husband. If y'all will excuse me a minute, I have a call on the boat that I need to return."

As Doc and Clyde boarded the *Obsession*, I trotted quickly back to my own boat. When I opened the salon hatch, Pescador was standing there waiting, still whining.

"Sorry, dude," Jimmy said. "I didn't want to yell across the dock that you had a call on your spy computer, man."

"What the hell's with that mutt?" Rusty said from the galley, where he and the forensics lady were talking. "Known that dog two years and he ain't never acted up like he has today."

"No clue," I said, opening the laptop. "Miss Stewart, Doc Fredric's here. They just went aboard to examine the bodies. If you'd like to help, I'm sure he'd appreciate it."

"Gunshots aren't my specialty, but I can take a hint," she replied with a bright smile, heading through the hatch.

After a second, Deuce's face appeared on the screen, with Julie standing over his shoulder. Thinking quickly, to let them know that Rusty was with me, I said, "How about making me some of whatever you're having, Rusty?"

Looking at me from the back of the laptop, my old friend winked as Deuce said, "Hold off on that a second, Rusty. I need to talk to Jesse in private, if you don't mind."

I nodded at Rusty and Jimmy, and the two headed for the hatch and out onto the dock, after Meg Stewart. "They're gone," I said. "What the hell is Stockwell doing, putting me in charge?"

"Just symbolic," Deuce said. "Actually, it was my idea. The whole team is up in Homestead, and Julie and I will get there before any of them can. So, since you were on the scene..."

"Well, at least it got you out of DC early. Can you tell me anything that I should pass on to the real investigators on the scene?"

Deuce gave me a complete rundown on the project the missing couple's company was working on. When he finished, I let out a low whistle. "An invisibility suit?"

"Not really invisibility," Julie said. "More like mimicry."

Then it hit me. The company's name. "Like a cephalopod? I get it now. Yeah, this thing would be extremely valuable on the battlefield."

"Which is why DHS and particularly the CCC has to be the lead investigative agency. If the Minniches have been abducted, this technology could end up in the hands of our enemies."

"How long till y'all get here?" I asked.

"We caught a tail wind most of the way and I told the pilot to keep it floored. We should be touching down in ten minutes. You're at City Marina?"

"Yeah, guess you'll surprise Rusty here, then?"

"He still doesn't know?" Julie asked.

"No, he and Jimmy stayed in the cockpit when we got here, watching after Pescador. Damn dog's been going nuts."

"Alright," Deuce said. "See you in about fifteen minutes."

I had to slide sideways through the hatch, to keep Pescador inside. Once I closed it, he erupted into continuous barking.

On the dock, I said to Jimmy, "Be careful going back in. He's right by the door."

"Why was Doc Fredric asking you if he could look at the stiffs?" Jimmy said.

"Stockwell put me in charge, until Deuce gets here."

"When's that gonna be?" Rusty asked.

"Come on, bro," I said. "We'll wait for them together. Should be here in twenty minutes or so."

When we rejoined the others at the stern of the large yacht, I noticed a crowd was gathering at the end of the dock and that another man had joined the group, waiting for the coroner and CSI team to finish up. He wore the same uniform as Marty, with captain's bars on his collar.

"You must be Captain Hammonds," I said.

"And you're Jesse McDermitt?" he asked. "I've heard of you around here. Never knew you were a Fed, though."

"We like to keep it that way," I said. "My boss will be here in just a few minutes. Until he arrives, you and your men are in charge of security here." Turning to Parsons, I said, "Can I talk to you a second, Dave?"

We walked out of earshot of the others and I turned toward him. "Have you seen this cephalopod suit? Is it as good as they say?"

"Better," he replied, unsurprised that I knew about it. "A guy was right in front of me wearing it, and I couldn't see him."

"I was a sniper instructor in the Corps, Dave. That's what we got paid to do."

"Yeah, but I bet you weren't lying on a table in a ghillie suit, with the table turning all psychedelic colors, were you?"

"Really? Damn, that'd be something to try out."

"How long have you had that dog of yours?" Parsons asked.

"Just over two years. Why?"

"I think we figured out what's got him so anxious," he replied, handing me a framed photograph.

In the photo the Minniches were standing on a deserted beach. I recognized them easily from the pictures Chyrel had shown me earlier. What I wasn't ready for was seeing a dog sitting next to Celia Minnich. A dog that looked exactly like Pescador.

"His name was Nadador," Parsons said. "It's Portuguese for swimmer. He belonged to Missus Minnich, a wedding gift from her husband. Nadador was swept overboard off the *Obsession* during Hurricane Wilma, two years ago."

"Son of a bitch," I mumbled. "That's exactly when we found him. Never could find the owner, though. So I called him Pescador, and he came to live with me."

"Pescador?"

"Spanish for fisherman. Long story. My late wife and I found him, stranded on a tiny island near mine, where he was surviving by catching fish."

"With a little luck," Parsons said, turning to return to the group, "we might have two happy endings. That is, if we can find the Minniches and return her dog to her."

The two crime scene investigators, along with Doc and his assistant, were still aboard the yacht when Deuce and Julie arrived ten minutes later. Rusty put on a good enough performance, then he and Julie went to my boat to catch up, along with Kim.

"Been too long," I said, taking Deuce's hand. "I know you gotta be glad to get out of DC."

"More than you know," he said. "I didn't realize how much I missed this stretch of rocks until we were on final approach and I could see the water. Did you get the boat opened up?"

"Yeah," I replied. "I had Dan take care of it." Dan Sullivan is a local musician and a friend of mine. After I introduced Deuce to the others, he addressed Binkowski first.

"While the disappearance of the Minniches does look like a kidnapping, Agent Binkowski, and I really believe it is, the national security implications of their work puts my team and Agent Parsons and his men at the forefront of the investigation. We will lean on you heavily for information you can provide through CODIS and any other sources you might have. Solving the kidnapping and getting the couple back have to be second to keeping certain information from getting into the wrong hands."

"The Bureau will help in any way we can, Agent Livingston."

Jimmy joined us, bringing my cellphone. "Heard it ringing," he said. "Took a few minutes, but I found it stuffed in the cushions of the settee. Good to see you, Deuce."

"Good to be seen, Jimmy," Deuce replied.

Looking at the caller ID, I saw that the missed call was from someone I hadn't talked to in a few months. Billy Rainwater had been a year behind me in school, but we'd been close growing up in Fort Myers. He'd followed me into the Marines after he graduated and we'd been stationed together a couple of times during his one tour.

"Someone you need to call back?" Deuce asked.

"It can wait," I replied. "An old friend from the mainland."

"I got this, Jesse. Go see to your dog. What's his problem, anyway?"

"Turns out he knows this yacht. Remember how Alex and I tried to find his owner for months? He used to belong to the Minniches."

"You're shitting me," he said, genuinely concerned. "Well, go check on him and return your call. You don't get many."

Linda followed me back toward the *Revenge*.

"Was it an important call?" Linda asked.

"Billy Rainwater, up in LaBelle," I replied.

I hit the call button. What Deuce said was true. I rarely received phone calls. Billy answered on the first ring. "Got something you might be interested in looking at, kemosabe."

Billy's a Seminole and not one to beat around the bush. He lives just east of Fort Myers, in the little town of LaBelle, on the Caloosahatchee River. He builds four-by-fours and buys and sells guns. Usually legally.

"Kinda busy right now, Billy. You at home?"

"Yeah. Well, I'm at the shop, that is. This is something you'll wanna take the time to see. Can you come up tomorrow?"

Looking back toward the growing group of people, I had the urge to do just that. A nice long drive away from the crowds, just me and Linda. Then my eyes fell on Waldrup, standing off to the side, watching and listening. He had his shades back on, though it was getting dark fast. Something told me he didn't miss much of anything. I'd promised him we'd find out who had killed his cousin, and I knew that with Deuce bringing the weight of a federal investigation, and all the resources he had at hand, it was a pretty done deal.

"I was planning to take my daughter flying tomorrow," I said.

"I'll meet you at the airport."

"About zero nine hundred?"

"Bring some cash," he replied. "About ten grand." I heard a click and looking at the screen, I saw the call had ended. Billy was never one for wasted words.

"We're flying up to LaBelle tomorrow?" Linda asked.

"Yeah, and you might have to look the other way about something."

"You don't know your friends as well as you think," she said, grinning.

"What's that supposed to mean?"

"William 'Walking Bear' Rainwater, Junior has worked with FDLE many times. He's a PI."

"Billy?" I asked, laughing. "A private investigator?"

"Paid informant," Linda corrected me. "He talks things up, like he's moving illegal arms, but everything he buys and sells is licensed and legal. Even the fifty-caliber machine gun he sold you."

"You're kidding," I said as I helped her across the gunwale. "I paid the smuggler's rate for that thing."

# CHAPTER FIFTEEN

ow the hell does he manage to manipulate me into these things?" I asked Linda when we stepped off the *Revenge* the next morning.

"Deuce doesn't manipulate, Dad," Kim said, following us up the dock toward the bar. "It's who you are."

"Who I was," I corrected her.

"No, it's who you are and always will be," Kim said. "If someone's in trouble and needs help, you just somehow end up being the one."

The two CSIs had worked gathering evidence well into the night. A couple of hours after sunset, while the CSIs were working, Deuce and I had sat down with the CID and FBI guys. Deuce had been impressed with the amount of knowledge the security man, Waldrup, had provided. He'd also been impressed enough by his stoic demeanor, considering he'd just identified the body of his cousin, that he'd invited Waldrup to sit in.

By then, Deuce had full files on both Waldrup and Parsons, as well as the Minniches and the Albrights. Neither couple had anything in their backgrounds that had jumped out at either of us before we sat down with the agents last night. It turned out that Waldrup was an Army Ranger first lieutenant. He'd been severely wounded in the liberation of Kuwait in 1991 and lost a leg just below the knee. This surprised me, as he didn't appear to be injured. During his recuperation, he'd been promoted to captain and discharged for medical reasons.

After we'd compared notes and Doc Fredric had confirmed the obvious cause of death of the couple on the yacht, I'd moved the *Revenge* over to Rusty's place. Mostly to get Pescador away from the scene. His constant whining and barking at every sound was a constant confirmation that it was him pictured with the couple in the photo Parsons had shown me.

I was now faced with the possibility that if the couple was found alive, I'd lose my dog. Pescador has been with me through a lot and actually killed a man who'd not only stabbed me, but was one of the ones who'd murdered my wife.

The CSIs hadn't come up with anything startling that we hadn't already known, or surmised. Parsons and Binkowski had agreed to meet us this morning at the *Anchor* to go over the CSI findings, so we'd called it a night just before midnight.

Holding the door open for Linda and Kim, I saw that both agents, along with Waldrup, were sitting at two large tables, pushed together in the corner. Marty and the forensics woman were there as well. Rusty brought another pot of coffee as the three of us sat down, Marty holding the chair next to him for Kim. The suspicious look Kim gave Meg Stewart didn't escape my attention.

A moment later, Captain Hammonds came in carrying a thick folder and sat down on Marty's other side, handing the folder to Deuce. "Got the report from our CSI team at four this morning. I've gone through everything. We matched prints found at the scene to both couples and all four crew, eliminating them. That left four unidentified sets of prints." He glanced quickly at Waldrup. "Also, two separate biological samples were gathered from the rape kit."

Turning back to Deuce, Hammonds said, "These guys didn't seem at all concerned that they were leaving evidence behind."

"They'd rigged the yacht to sink," I said. "Taking any evidence with it."

Binkowski cleared his throat. "Both the unidentified prints and the DNA samples were sent to our crime lab in Miami. A priority message from the SecDef put this evidence at the top of the list, but it'll still be a day or two at least on the DNA."

Hammonds glanced around the table, lingering on Kim for a moment before looking at me. "Do you think it wise to have your daughter here?"

I was about to put the man in his place, when Linda forcefully said, "Captain Hammonds, Miss McDermitt is a student at UF, studying criminal justice. When she graduates, she'll come to work at FDLE. I'll vouch for her sitting in."

"Very well," Hammonds replied, obviously unaccustomed to having his chain jerked by a woman. "Through Doctor Fredric's report, assisted by Miss Stewart here, the blood samples were analyzed and compared to the known blood types of the Minniches. Mister Minnich is

A negative, pretty rare, less than six in a hundred people. None of the samples matched his. Missus Minnich is AB negative, the rarest blood type. Fewer than one in a hundred people have this. There was a small pool of blood found on the deck in the main cabin area, just behind the helm. The splatter was smudged and foreign particles were mixed with it. The sample was identified as AB negative and the foreign traces were determined to be from an expensive brand of lipstick. Sergeant Jimenez is our blood splatter expert. He reports that the smudged sample was likely caused when Missus Minnich was struck and fell to the floor, her lipstick mixing with the blood."

"Based on the CSIs' findings," Binkowski began, "the Bureau feels certain the Minniches have been kidnapped and are possibly still alive. The director has met with the Homeland secretary and promised complete and full disclosure of any Bureau findings."

Deuce turned to me. "Jesse, you're flying up to LaBelle this morning. What's the range of your plane?"

"You have a plane?" Waldrup asked.

"Yeah. It's a fifty-three Beaver floatplane. And yeah, we're leaving inside an hour. It can fly four hundred and fifty miles, Deuce. Why?"

"I'm going with you. We'll refuel in LaBelle, and after your business there is concluded, you're going to fly me over the Cay Sal Bank."

"That's just gonna have to sit on the back burner," I said. "I promised Waldrup we'd find out who did this."

"There's a chance they're connected," Deuce replied.

Thinking that over for a moment, and knowing Deuce wasn't a speculative kind of man, I said, "Okay, who else is going?"

"I am," Parsons and Binkowski said at the same time.

"Only one of you," Deuce said. "Captain Waldrup will be joining us, and there's only room for one more."

"You go," Binkowski said to Parsons. "I'll drive up to the crime lab and see if I can push the prints any faster."

"Alright," Deuce said. "Anything else, Captain Hammonds?"

"I find it unusual to have this kind of discussion in a bar," Hammonds said, looking around. Rusty, Julie, and Jimmy sat at the bar drinking coffee and watching the Weather Channel. Yesterday's rain was late getting here, blowing through in the middle of the night.

"Captain," Deuce said, "Jimmy over there is first mate on the *Revenge* and has accompanied us on a number of missions. The woman sitting next to him is my wife, a Coast Guard petty officer and a valued member of my team. Rusty is my father-in-law and former Force Recon Marine. As a federal agent, I wouldn't have any trouble speaking openly in front of any of them."

"It's like I told you, Captain," Marty said. "Locals down here are like family, and in a lot of cases we are family. You'll get used to it."

Hammonds glanced at Marty, then said, "No, that's pretty much it on the findings, until the FBI gets back to us on the results of the prints and DNA analysis."

Rising, I looked at Waldrup. "Center row, port side."

"I'm sorry, sir?"

"To offset Deuce's and my weight in the plane. And if you call me sir one more time, I'll pull your leg off and beat you with it."

The big man looked up at me from his chair and grinned. "Just what will we be looking for, Gunny?"

"Beats me," I replied, looking over at Deuce. "Ask the AIC."

"We've had reports of black marketers working out of the Cay Sal Bank," Deuce told him. "In Jesse's plane, we can fly low and slow. If we see anyone out there, you just might have seen them around CephaloTech and can let us know."

"What are the odds of that?" Waldrup asked, standing up.

"Jesse and I are pretty good at sizing men up, Captain. Tell me something. What's the registration number on Jesse's boat?"

"FL one three eight seven KW," he replied with a grin. "It's a gift I've always had."

"Exactly," Deuce said, heading to the bar to get a couple of thermoses filled and say goodbye to Julie.

Meg glanced up at the big man and smiled. "I don't think Mister McDermitt was serious about breaking your leg off."

"Pull it off, ma'am," he corrected her. "It's a prosthetic. I left the real one in Kuwait."

"Really?" she replied, looking down at his feet. Waldrup hitched up his right trouser leg slightly, exposing his prosthetic. "I never would have guessed it."

Kim and Marty went outside to say goodbye, and Meg turned to me. "You don't have room for one more, do you?"

Seeing Binkowski already halfway to the door, I glanced at Deuce, who nodded slightly. I grinned at the smallish woman. "I think you might fit in the boot."

Twenty minutes later, with Kim at the controls, we taxied down the ramp and into the water. The deHavilland Beaver is a true bush plane. There are still hundreds in service today all over the world. Its ability to lift plenty of cargo and passengers into the air from a short airstrip, lake, or snow-covered pasture is legendary. Mine has WipAire floats, with landing gear that retracts into the pontoons.

Kim raised the landing gear and bumped the throttle up a little as we taxied to deeper water. The wind had changed from the north to the usual easterly breeze and she turned into it, getting clearance from air traffic control at Marathon Airport.

Lining up with the entrance marker to Vaca Cut, Kim pushed the throttle lever forward. The big engine roared as it pulled the *Hopper's* floats up onto plane and accelerated across Vaca Key Bight.

"When you said you had a plane," Waldrup's voice came over my headset, "I thought you meant you were the pilot."

I looked back to where Waldrup sat on the opposite side and grinned. "I'm a pilot. Kim's still taking classes, but will have her license in a month."

In the time of that short conversation, *Island Hopper* reached takeoff speed and Kim gently pulled back on the yoke. The ascent was nice and even, as she banked to the south to avoid flying over Key Colony Beach.

"Very smooth," I said. "You're getting better. Once you circle around Key Colony, head north over Long Point Key. LaBelle is just a few degrees west of due north."

Kim nodded and slowly banked the plane to the left as we continued to climb, the big Pratt and Whitney radial engine pulling the load effortlessly. "You're gonna land, right?" Kim asked. "I'm okay on the bay here, but landing on a river I'm not so sure about."

"We're landing at the airport. It's a short strip and will be good practice."

Deuce sat directly behind me, across from Waldrup. Linda, Meg, and the CID man had the wide rear seat. Parsons was looking out the window at the long island chain extending to the far-off horizon. "You know, I've never been down here. It looks a lot different from up in the sky. You don't really appreciate that you're on an island down there. What kind of business do you have in LaBelle?"

I glanced back at Linda and she nodded slightly. "I'm meeting a gun dealer friend of mine. He has something he thinks I might want to buy."

"Agent Livingston?" Waldrup asked. "What makes you think the black marketers down near Cuba are involved in the Minniches' disappearance?"

"Cuba?" Dave asked. "I thought the Cay Sal Bank was in the Bahamas."

"It's part of the Bahamas," Deuce explained. "But the distance from there to Cuba is a third of the distance to the next nearest Bahamian island." Then to Waldrup, he said, "You gotta call me Deuce, okay, Miguel? To answer your question, nothing I've heard points to their involvement. It's just a hunch. These black marketers can come and go from the little keys that make up the Bank without any kind of intervention from Havana, and it's well outside our territorial waters. In fact, Castro approves of black marketing. We have wiretaps on a number of phones these people are using, mostly Russians, and since the day before yesterday, they've gone almost completely silent. I'm not big on coincidences."

Less than an hour later, I switched to the small LaBelle Airport frequency and keyed the mic. "Labelle Unicorn, this is deHavilland November one three eight five, ten miles south for landing."

After a moment, and no response, I repeated our intentions. Any air traffic arriving or departing would be on this frequency, as it was an unmanned airport. So, I told Kim to turn northwest and begin her landing checklist. Five minutes later, she banked right and made a 180-degree turn. On final approach, she lowered the landing gear, reduced power, and added fifteen degrees of flap.

"The wind's real light," I said. "But it's a bit of a crosswind. You'll feel the plane kinda jerk left, when the wheels touch down. It won't be much of a jerk, but be ready for it and just give her a little right rudder."

Kim nodded, bringing the speed down a little more as she watched the runway ahead of us. "How long's the runway?"

"Over five thousand feet," I replied. "You won't need half of it."

A few minutes later, after a nearly perfect landing, we taxied toward the fixed base operator's building. I could see Billy waiting just outside the door, wearing his typical western shirt and jeans, his black hair pulled back in a long ponytail.

I left Deuce and Kim to take care of securing the plane and arranging for fuel. Linda and I strode toward my old friend. If he was surprised to see Linda, he didn't show it.

"Agent Rosales," Billy said with a nod. "I didn't expect you to be coming."

He shook hands with her and she said, "I'm not here in any official capacity, Billy. Jesse and I have been seeing each other for several months."

When Billy turned to me, we grasped forearms, shaking hands the Seminole way. "Good to see you again, kemosabe. Are you chartering people in the plane now?"

"Just some friends," I replied as Kim came trotting up. "And my daughter. Billy, meet Kim. Kim, this is one of my oldest friends, Billy Rainwater. We've known each other since before kindergarten."

Billy looked from Kim to me and back again as a slow grin crept across his usually stoic features. "I remember when you were born," he said, giving her a hug. "Damn, I must be getting old." Then he turned to me. "I only brought my pickup."

"The others will wait here," I said. "Just Linda and I are going with you to the shop."

"Deuce already paid for the gas, Dad," Kim said. "He wouldn't let me use your card."

"Okay, head back and keep them company, check the plane out and make sure she's ready for takeoff."

Linda and I followed Billy through the small terminal and outside. Parked at the curb was his burly K5 Blazer, sitting on huge tires and monster suspension. "How's that old Travelall running?" he asked as I helped Linda climb up into the truck.

"Like it was new," I replied. "Are you going to tell me what it is you want to sell me?"

"No," he replied, his face an inscrutable mask once more.

He turned right on Cowboy Way and drove a few hundred feet, then turned left on Forrey Drive, before he spoke again. "I wanna see the look on your face when you see it."

Just a mile later, he turned onto Highway 80, headed east away from town. The powerful engine pushed the big truck quickly to sixty, the giant tires making a loud humming sound on the pavement. A mile down the road, Billy turned left off the highway and into the gravel parking area at his shop. The doors were all closed. He parked the truck and the three of us went inside, Billy leading the way to the back of the building.

"No work today?" I asked.

"Not today, Jesse," he replied, looking back and grinning. "I'm planning to make some big bucks off a white man."

At the rear of the garage, he pulled a tarp off a stack of boxes. The wooden box on top was about three feet long and eight inches on the sides. Billy undid the clasps and tossed the lid up.

Letting out a low whistle, I looked up at my old hunting buddy, standing next to Linda. "Is that what I think it is?"

Billy grinned. "If you think it's an M134 minigun, yeah."

"You have the motor and battery for it?" I asked, inspecting the electrically operated Gatling-type machine gun. The minigun dates back to when Richard Gatling replaced his hand crank with a newly invented electric motor. The modern version is used in close air support from helicopters. It has six barrels that spin and chew up ammo at an alarming speed. It could empty a twenty-five-hundred-round ammo can in under a minute.

"I have the motors, no batteries."

"Motors? As in a spare?"

Billy grinned. "No, kemosabe. Motors, as in one for the gun and one for the ammo feed."

"Why two?" I asked, puzzled.

"In a chopper," Billy explained, "the gun's mounted low to the deck, with the ammo can mounted off to the side. I built a custom feed assembly, to help pull the belt out of a can mounted lower, under the pedestal. With the two motors working together, it'll fire five thousand rounds per minute."

"You're kidding! That'll melt the barrels."

"Not this one," Billy said. "Barrels are heavy-bore titanium, just like the mount for your Ma Deuce."

"Think you can build a mount for it that'll adapt to that tripod?" Almost a year ago, I'd bought an M2 fifty-caliber machine gun from Billy. He'd custom built a titanium mount with a center post that fit into the fighting chair mount on the *Revenge's* cockpit deck. It had three legs that folded out and rested on the deck with rubber pads. The thing was extremely stable. At least, it was as stable a platform as you could have with a Ma Deuce. The recoil of the big gun made accurate shooting on automatic virtually impossible without using tracer rounds.

Kicking the edge of the tarp back further with the toe of his cowboy boot, he bent down and opened a second, much larger square box. "Already did. Everything you need, except the batteries. You'll have to find a coupla twenty-five-volt aircraft batteries for that."

Linda hadn't said anything. I glanced at her, and one corner of her mouth turned up slightly. Turning back to Billy, I asked, "How much?"

# CHAPTER SIXTEEN

Half an hour later, with my new minigun and mount loaded behind the backseats, we were airborne again and headed south. Deuce leaned forward and with his hand over the mic boom on his headset asked what I'd paid for the minigun. I held up seven fingers.

"You paid what?" Deuce asked incredulously, his hand coming away from the mic.

"I need to take Linda with me whenever I buy illegal weapons," I replied.

"It wasn't illegal," Linda said. "While you were loading it in the truck, I checked and saw that Billy's collector licenses and permits were all up to date."

"But he would have asked a lot more than the eight grand," I said. "If he didn't know the sale was okay in your eyes."

"Yeah, and your counteroffer would have been a lot higher, too."

"What do you need a gun like that for, anyway?" Meg asked over the intercom.

I turned and started to say something, when Kim interrupted me. "It's not a matter of need," she said. "In this country, we can have as many of any kind of weapons as we want."

"Oh, please don't get me wrong," Meg said. "I have absolutely nothing against your Second Amendment right. I shoot as well. I was only wondering what a person who would own a gun like that might be afraid of."

Kim glanced over at me and grinned as the *Hopper* leveled off at five thousand feet. "Not a damned thing," she said.

Parsons continued to look out the window as we flew over the Everglades, seemingly lost in thought. I'd turned around and was talking with Miguel and Deuce, figuring out all the many places we'd been and where we might have crossed wakes. While we talked, I watched the CID man.

Though Parsons was looking out the window, he wasn't looking down as most people would. The view was spectacular as we flew out over Florida Bay, leaving the mainland behind us.

The water of Florida Bay is well known for how crystal clear it is. It's less salty than the Gulf or Atlantic, due to the influx of fresh water, filtered through the hundreds of square miles that make up the Glades. Small patch reefs and tiny islands and shoals dot the huge bay. A bit less interesting, the cobalt waters of the Gulf could be seen to the west. But it was the horizon that Parsons seemed to be studying. Or more accurately, ignoring. He was obviously deep in thought.

As we flew over the Keys a few minutes later, Parsons turned and leaned forward in his seat. "You're sure these black marketers are Russian?"

Deuce thought for a moment. "I've heard some of the tapes. They definitely speak Russian, but you're right, they could be any nationality."

Parsons frowned. "So they could be from any Russian-speaking country? Ukraine, or maybe Belarus?"

"Possibly," Deuce said. "I speak a little Russian. Hate the language. I read the transcripts of the calls that a Russian-language translator made."

"Not a linguist?" Parsons asked. "There are some very subtle differences, ya know. Much like the Spanish spoken in South America is a little different than the Spanish spoken in South Florida."

"You speak Russian?" I asked.

Parsons glanced at me. "I don't speak any language other than English. And even that's Southern English. Oh, I've picked up a word or two of other languages here and there. But, I've always had a good ear for regional accents of the people I worked with. Guess thirty years in the Army'll do that. And even though I can't understand what a Russian or Azerbaijani is saying, I can usually pick up which is which."

Deuce produced a small case from his jacket pocket and handed it to Parsons. Inside was a miniature communications device that attached to and was inserted in the ear. The mic on what we usually called an earwig was in the end of the part that went around the ear. It was held tightly in place against the back of the jawbone and picked up sound through the thin skin there as it resonated off the bone.

"Put that on for a minute," Deuce said as he handed me another earwig. We each pulled one side of our headphones away and put the small devices on, covering them again with the comparatively bulky headphones. I switched off the intercom and we checked the link between the three earwigs. Then Deuce took his phone out and sent a text message.

After a moment, I heard a beep from the earwig and then a familiar voice. "Hey, boss," Chyrel said. "All three are connected through your phone. What's up?"

"Jesse and CID Agent Parsons are on with us, Chyrel," Deuce said by way of reply. "I need you to pull up a secure audio file and play it for us."

He gave her the file name and location on the DHS secure server and a moment later we listened to a conversation in Russian. I knew a few words and phrases, but didn't recognize anything that was said.

"I don't think that's Russian Russian," Parsons said, when the recording ended. "My bet would be Turkmenistan. I spent three months there on a murder investigation involving a soldier."

Deuce nodded and grinned at me. "Chyrel," he said. "Send that recording to Kumar. Tell him to get with one of his Delta buddies who knows multiple Russian dialects. Get back to me when you have something."

Kumar Sayef is the leader of the CCC team in Key Largo and a good friend. A former sergeant first class and an interpreter for the Army's covert Delta Force, he'd been with Deuce's team for over a year. Kumar only recently took over command of the new team.

I switched the intercom back on to allow the others to speak, but after less than five minutes, Kumar's voice came over the earwig and I switched the intercom off again.

"Hiya, Deuce," Kumar said. Though he was of Middle Eastern descent, he was actually born and raised in the upper Midwest. He spoke many languages and dialects fluently, but his natural voice had that Fargo kind of twang to it.

"That was fast, Kumar," Deuce said. "Did you find out anything?"

"Yeah, it just happens that I'm at Bragg right now, talking to an Arabic linguist about his future. It only took him a minute to get the right guy in the office. The conversation Chyrel sent me is definitely the Turkmen dialect of Russian that's spoken in Turkmenistan and a few other places. The accent of both speakers is probably the Balkan Province on the Caspian Sea. Is this about that black market ring down in the Cay Sal Bank?"

"Yeah, it is. I should have had it authenticated by someone that knows the dialects. How sure is your guy?"

"Absolutely one hundred percent that it's Turkmen Russian, and he's pretty certain on the provincial accents. Call it ninety percent."

"Thanks, Kumar," Deuce said and ended the call. Parsons removed the earwig as I switched the intercom back on. When he started to hand it back, Deuce told him to hang onto it for the time being.

"That conversation was between the leader of the black marketers and one of his men," Deuce explained. "It was recorded about a week ago, and they were discussing the acquisition of the plans for a piece of hardware to sell to their neighbor."

"What countries border Turkmenistan?" Linda asked.

"A few of the other Stans, mostly," I replied, looking at Deuce, both of us frowning. "Afghanistan, Kazakhstan, and Uzbekistan."

"And Iran to the south," Deuce added, finishing my thought.

# CHAPTER SEVENTEEN

Delores Juarez was working at her desk when her phone buzzed. The flashing light indicated the call was from the security gate. With Miguel down in the Keys liaising with Agent Parsons as the go-between for the company, Delores was having security calls routed to her.

Pushing the button, she asked, "What is it?"

"Sergeant Gonzales here," the gate guard said unnecessarily. Delores knew who was on duty in every position within the company. "There's an unscheduled UPS delivery for you at the gate. A letter-sized envelope."

"I'm not expecting anything. Who is it from?"

"It doesn't say, ma'am. No return address. The driver's scan says it was picked up from a drop box in Coconut Grove."

Delores thought for a moment. "Have Peter take it to the security office. I'll be down there in five minutes."

The company rarely received unscheduled deliveries of any kind. UPS deliveries usually consisted of several boxes of assorted office materials. She rose and left her office, taking the elevator to the basement office of the company's security team.

Peter Timmons, the other security guard on duty at the gate, boarded the elevator at the lobby level. He held the envelope in both hands, as if it were made of fragile glass.

"What do you think it is, Miss Juarez?"

"Looks like a letter," she replied. "But, as you know, all unscheduled deliveries have to go through security screening."

CephaloTech had received a few letters from irate liberals living in the area. They were usually antimilitary and anti-big business, accusing the company of everything from building nuclear weapons to discharging toxic waste into the city's water supply.

When the door opened at the security office lobby, Delores and Peter walked past the guard at the desk and Delores used her card to open the panel next to a heavy door. Pressing her thumb onto the panel, she unlocked the door, pushed it open, and stepped into the heart of the company's security hub.

Twenty minutes later, after the envelope had undergone a number of tests, including X-ray, it was deemed harmless and Delores took it back to her office.

At her desk, Delores slid a letter opener into the flap and gently cut it open. Inside, she found a single sheet of paper. When she pulled it out, she knew without reading it that it would be an important clue to Agent Parsons's investigation.

Picking up the business card that Parsons had given her from her desk, she quickly dialed the number.

She could barely hear Parsons's voice when he answered on the third ring, a loud roaring in the background all but drowning him out.

"I can hardly hear you," Delores said. "Where are you?"

"In a really noisy airplane," his shouted reply came.

"We just received a ransom letter. It came to the office just a few minutes ago."

"A ransom letter?" Parsons asked. "Look, I can barely hear you, can you scan or photograph it and send it to me?"

"Right away," Delores replied and ended the call.

Placing the letter on her desk, she turned the desk lamp brighter and used the camera function of her cell phone to make a high-resolution digital image of the paper. Quickly, she attached the image to a text message and sent it.

A moment later, she received a reply from the CID agent, telling her that he'd received it. He also told her not to handle it and he'd have someone there from the FBI as soon as possible.

Sitting at her desk again, she examined the letter, turning it with the eraser end of a pencil. It looked like regular notebook paper, with words and letters cut from magazines or books and glued in place. The sender wanted two and a half million dollars and would send another letter the following day with details on when and where the delivery was to be made.

Half an hour later, Delores's phone buzzed again. She saw that it was the security gate again. "What is it, Rodrigo?" she asked when she pushed the button.

"An FBI agent to see you, ma'am," Sergeant Rodrigo Gonzales replied. "Special Agent William Binkowski."

"Tell him I'll meet him in the lobby. And call there and have them buzz him in."

A few minutes later, the elevator door opened and she walked across the lobby to where a middle-aged man in an inexpensive business suit stood by the security desk.

As she approached, he held out his credentials to her. "Special Agent William Binkowski, FBI."

Delores took the ID and badge from him. She examined it and compared the face on it to the man in front of her. Satisfied, she handed the ID back to him. "My name is Delores Juarez, Agent Binkowski. I'm the chief of operations here at CephaloTech. Will you follow me, please?"

Together they went up to her office on the second floor. "It's right there on the desk," she said, leading him into her office.

"Have you touched it?" Binkowski asked, pulling on a pair of latex gloves.

"Yes," she replied. "I pulled it out of the envelope. My finger prints will be on the top, near the center."

Binkowski placed a briefcase on her desk and opened it. From inside, he removed two clear plastic evidence bags and a felt-tip marker. Before doing anything else, he recorded the date and time on the appropriate lines on the back of the evidence bags.

Taking a small digital camera from his briefcase, Binkowski photographed the letter, the envelope and the desk itself, with the two evidence bags on it. Using tweezers, he first picked up the envelope the letter came in and turned it over, showing the address label.

"How many people handled this envelope?" Binkowski asked.

Delores thought for a moment. "At least five since it arrived here. Unscheduled deliveries go through a security screening before being delivered to the recipient."

Glancing at the label, Binkowski said, "It's addressed specifically to you. By name." He picked the envelope up again and placed it in one of the evidence bags before turning his attention to the letter itself. "You're sure that you're the only one to touch the letter itself?"

"Yes, I opened it right here at my desk and when I took it out, I called Agent Parsons immediately. He told me to not touch it and wait for you."

"That's good," Binkowski said. "We might be able to get something off of this. I assume your prints are on file with your security department?"

"They are," Delores replied. "As are all our employees'."

"Will you be able to get the two and a half million together on such short notice?"

"You think we should pay the ransom?" Delores asked.

Straightening, Binkowski looked at her. "That wasn't what I asked, ma'am. Two and a half million dollars is a lot of money, and a pretty specific amount. The sender may know how much money your company has available on short notice."

"Oh," Delores said. "Yes, we can put together that amount of cash in short order."

"More than that?"

"Not much more," she replied. Crossing her arms, Delores moved toward the window and looked out. "Very few people know that."

"Who does?"

Delores turned back to Binkowski. "Myself, and the Minniches, of course. Our head of security, Captain Waldrup, knows everything there is to know at CephaloTech. Then, maybe two people in our financial office."

Glancing at the UPS envelope, Binkowski said, "This was picked up at a drop box yesterday evening, in Coconut Grove. I was with Waldrup since about three in the afternoon. Those boxes have pickups every four hours, so that rules him out. Obviously, the kidnapped couple is out, too."

"I've been here since yesterday morning," Delores said. "Security records will show that."

"Can I examine the employee records of the two people in financial, along with their time cards or whatever?"

"Of course," Delores replied. "But they're not cards. Access to the plant is through scanned security cards and a fingerprint scanner, all records stored electronically. I'll send for the files."

# CHAPTER EIGHTEEN

Crossing the Gulf Stream, I told Kim to drop down under five hundred. The last thing I wanted was to get picked up on Cuban radar and have some trigger-happy radar operator scramble a couple of MiG fighters. Way in the distance, I could just make out the color change of the water at the northern edge of Cay Sal Bank.

Parsons pulled his sat phone from his jacket pocket. "Hey, I need to take this call. Any way to make the engine noise quieter?"

I turned to Kim and said, "Throttle back and go into a slight descent to maintain speed."

The result was quieter, but still loud, as Parsons answered the phone. He told the caller he was in a plane and then listened for a minute, before saying, "A ransom letter? Look, I can barely hear you, can you scan or photograph it and send it to me?"

Parsons ended the call, and a moment later, he checked the screen on his phone. He studied it for a minute before typing with his thumbs on the tiny keyboard.

"Take a look at this," Parsons said, handing his phone to Deuce. "What do you make of it?"

Leaning forward, Deuce held Parsons's phone so I could see it. Someone had cut individual letters from magazines to create a ransom demand.

"Guess that answers the question of whether or not they were kidnapped," I said.

"Not really," Parsons muttered. "And this compounds things." I was confused, and I guess it showed on my face. "Anyone who knows the Minniches are missing could have sent that. I need to send Agent Binkowski over to the CephaloTech office."

"Already on it," Deuce said, his fingers flying on his phone's keypad.

"Oh," Parsons said, looking up from his phone at Deuce. Then he continued explaining his thought to me. "Anyway, Binkowski will likely start digging to find out how many people know of their disappearance. Usually a letter like that, with stuff cut from magazines, that's the sign of an amateur. These days, you can write the letter on your phone, duck into an Internet café just about any-where in the country and send it wirelessly to a cheap la-ser printer to make a hard copy for just a buck, that'd be almost untraceable. I don't think that letter came from the people that took the yacht down at sea. That was done by pros."

"How many do you think know about the kidnap-ping?" I asked. "Are all of them suspect?"

"Less than half a dozen," Waldrup cut in.

Parsons nodded at the big man. "I told your COO up there to not let it out as public knowledge. Binkows-ki will find out, I'm sure. And he'll probably start imme-diately on eliminating suspects. But if my hunch is right, the letter wasn't sent by the people who have the Minn-iches."

"Can I throttle up and climb now, Dad?"

I turned and looked forward, seeing we were below three hundred feet. I gently increased throttle for her and said, "Drop on down to about two fifty and keep the speed about a hundred knots." Pointing ahead and to the left, I added, "There's the old Elbow Cay lighthouse. Turn left and follow the edge of the bank."

"Whoa!" Kim said. "It's beautiful. How deep's the water?"

"The bank is shallow. Ten feet or so, most of it. The deepest parts are only forty or fifty feet. Outside the ring of cays and shoals, it drops fast to over three hundred, then eighteen hundred a little further out."

We flew low and slow, two hundred and fifty feet above the waves and a few hundred feet out from the shallows. A few dilapidated shells of old houses could be seen on Elbow Cay, along with the ruins of the old lighthouse. Stunted palm trees and dwarf pines tried to gain a foothold on the rocky ground.

"People used to live there?" Linda asked as we all watched out the starboard windows, looking for any sign of life.

"The light keeper and a few others," I replied. "It'd be a really hard life, though, being so far from anywhere."

"You make it look easy on your island," Linda said.

"That's different. My island's only a ten-minute boat ride, across calm water, to a store on Big Pine. Out here, it's thirty miles to Cuba, sixty miles to the Keys, and seventy-five miles to the nearest Bahamian island. All across very deep water, with treacherous shoals and currents."

We continued flying along the chain of mostly submerged islands for twenty minutes, until we reached the Dog Rocks on the northeast corner of the triangular atoll.

"Turn and follow the string south," I told Kim. "Are you comfortable flying lower? I don't want the Cubans to get all excited. We'll be near their radar range soon."

"A hundred feet?"

"That's my girl," I replied. Then I turned in my seat and said to the others, "Keep your eyes peeled. We're dropping down to the wave tops. The islands along this side are really small for a while, most not even big enough for a gull to stand one-legged on."

Kim was very steady on the controls, watching the horizon ahead and keeping a close eye on the altimeter, as the big radial engine droned on and on toward the Cuban coast, just over the horizon.

Passing Dangerous Shoals and Bellows Cay, Waldrup said he thought he saw someone on the tiny cay. "Circle left," I said to Kim. "Then come across the is-land east–west and finish a figure eight to the right, if we don't see anything."

As we passed directly over the tiny rock outcrop-ping, flying low, Waldrup said, "No, it's just a dead tree."

Kim began the turn to the right to circle around and line back up with the eastern edge of the bank. "There's something unusual," Meg said from the back. I looked where she was pointing but didn't see anything.

"What was it?" I asked.

"I'm not entirely certain," Meg replied. "To the right of that next group of islands, it looked like a boat or something. In close to the trees, but obscured by them."

"That's Anguilla Cay," I said. "The west side is most-ly a tidal flat, with a couple of sand beaches, but most-ly rocks." To Kim, I added, "It's the southern tip of Cay Sal Bank. When we get past it, turn northwest and keep following the edge of the bank. We'll be able to see the whole western shore of Anguilla Cay as we head up to the last few islands on the west side."

"What's that?" Linda asked excitedly.

"Looks like a shack of some kind," Waldrup said as I heard the clicking of Deuce's high-speed camera.

Sure enough, back among the low trees and brush in the middle of South Anguilla Cay, I could just make out a low structure. It looked like someone had taken great pains to conceal it, but they didn't do a very good job on the metal roof, which reflected sunlight through the palm fronds on top of it.

As the *Hopper* banked steeply around the south end of the island, Meg shouted excitedly, "There! It *is* a boat!"

In a small cove, just west of where the shack was, a good-sized commercial fishing boat was stranded on the sand and laying over slightly on its port side. It wasn't unusual to see derelict vessels on Cay Sal Bank, but this one didn't look like it'd been there long. Nor did it look like it was abandoned. The rifle barrel sticking out of the pilothouse window told me there was at least one person aboard.

"My aircraft!" I shouted, grabbing the wheel.

Kim released hers instantly. "Your aircraft."

I jammed the throttle to the stop and banked sharply left while putting the *Hopper* into a steep dive, gaining speed.

The big radial protested as I pulled back on the yoke and banked hard right, putting us into a steep, climbing turn. Someone yelled something, but I was too busy taking evasive action. At four hundred feet, I put *Island Hopper* back over on her left side, diving once more for the water's surface. At the last second, I leveled off, the pontoons just a few feet off the water.

"What the hell are you doing?" Deuce shouted.

Looking out the window and back toward the island, I saw that we were now a good mile away and started a slow climb, banking to a northerly heading.

"That wasn't a derelict vessel," I said. "Take the controls, Kim. Make your course three one five degrees. We're headed home."

When Kim took the yoke, I turned around in my seat. "Is anyone hit?"

"Hit?" Parsons asked.

"Yeah," Waldrup said. "You got a hole in your plane and I got a hole in my leg. Fortunately, it's the one that's replaceable."

"Someone was shooting at us?" Deuce asked. "I didn't see anyone."

"He was in the pilothouse," I said. "Leaning out a porthole with a rifle."

Waldrup pointed just in front of where Deuce was sitting. "Missed you by just a few inches, Agent Livingston." Then he pulled up the cuff of his trousers, extending his right leg out into the narrow aisle between the seats. "If I'd been wearing my old plastic prosthetic, you guys would be helping me outta this plane when we land. Titanium ain't cheap."

Imbedded in the gray titanium rod just above the articulated ankle joint was what looked like the mushroomed remains of a bullet. "Linda," I said. "There's a small toolbox strapped under your seat. Hand Deuce the needlenose pliers."

When she passed them up, Deuce bent over and, with some effort, extracted the bullet from Waldrup's fake leg. He held it up so I could get a better look.

"Small caliber," Deuce said. "Probably five-point-five-six."

I reached out and turned his hand for a better look. "Looks a bit smaller than that."

"Smaller?" Deuce asked.

"I've shot a lot of M16 rounds, brother."

Parsons reached forward with a small plastic bag he held open. Deuce dropped the bullet in and Parsons sealed it, then wrote something on the white label before holding it up to examine it more closely.

"What did the weapon look like?" Parsons asked me, as if making small talk, while stuffing the little evidence bag in his jacket pocket.

I thought for a moment. "Black or gray assault rifle," I replied. "Probably composite. Definitely not wood, like an AK. But it didn't look like an American AR type either. It had a forward-curving magazine, and the gas block was forward of the grip."

"You have a good eye, Jesse," Parsons said. "The Russians began manufacturing a low-recoil assault rifle more than ten years ago. It's chambered for their five-point-four-five round. It was supposed to replace the AK74, but due to the high cost of production, Nikonov shut down production of the AN94 just last year."

"How many were manufactured?" Deuce asked.

"Several thousand," Parsons replied. "Not all are still with the police and military, though."

"Ties in with your black marketers," I told Deuce.

"Anyone see anything else?" Parsons asked.

"I'll know more when I can plug my camera's memory card into a computer," Deuce said.

"He shot my damned plane," I said, barely audibly. *With my daughter and girlfriend aboard*, I thought. *Somebody's gonna pay.*

# CHAPTER NINETEEN

Darius had a backdoor into his company's computer system that only he knew about. "Do we have an agreement?" he asked Dobrovska, as he sat at the small table, ready to access the company's mainframe.

Ilya stared at Darius for a moment. "Cut her down, as well, Oleg." He then put the pistol away and squatted down in front of Darius. "Do you realize what you're bargaining away?"

"I'm not stupid, Mister Dobrovska. Once I give you what you want, I'm a traitor to my country and there's nothing to stop you from killing us. But there are a few other things your clients might be interested in. Things that could have made me a very rich man in America. Better a slightly rich man living as a traitor in exile, than dead."

A smile slowly spread across Ilya's face. "What you are offering will indeed make you a traitor to your country."

"All I ask is that my wife and I be allowed to live. I don't see that I have much choice. You have nothing to gain by releasing us after you get what you want."

"What exactly are you offering?" Ilya asked as Celia came over to stand behind her husband, tying her shirt-tail into a knot below her bosom.

"The technology you want was designed to be thwarted, just in case one of the suits fell into the wrong hands," Darius replied. "Your clients can probably produce a working model within a month or two, using the technology I will give you. It will work flawlessly and they will be very appreciative. Until the Pentagon finds out that it's been stolen. Once your client builds it, you can then sell them additional information, along with the location in the millions of lines of code where the disable command is buried."

"And why should I trust that this *disable command* even exists or that you will deliver it?" Ilya asked.

"We have nothing to lose but our lives," Darius replied. "You sell them the technology and let them build it. I'll already be a traitor then and wanted by my government. We can never go back to America. But you can take us somewhere where we can live comfortably. Once your client builds the suit, they'll see that it's worth far more than they paid for it and will gladly pay for the coding. That information, I'll keep to myself until we're set up safe somewhere. What you sell the information for, I get half."

Dobrovska considered it a moment. "What's to stop Oleg from turning your wife into a one-armed whore, if you don't give it to me now?"

"Nothing but the knowledge that I could give you the wrong information, and with us dead, you'll never get the correct coding. It would take your clients years to locate the single line of code, if they could find it at all. When the American military makes their suit useless, your clients will want to talk to you. Look, I'm a businessman, just like you. Once they manufacture the first suit and test it, they'll gladly pay ten times more for the coding to make it invulnerable."

Ilya rose quickly. "You must be hungry. You have not eaten in two days. Thirsty, as well, I suspect. Oleg, bring the computer. We will go to the boat, where our new business partners will be more comfortable."

As Ilya walked toward the door, Oleg closed the laptop and put it in the bag. Darius could hardly believe that his ploy was working. The coding was there—that was a stipulation the Pentagon had insisted on. Without knowing what to look for or where to look, whoever was buying the technology would never find it. Darius had had his doubts about whether his plan would work, but dangling more dollars in front of the man seemed to do the trick.

Rising from the now-empty desk, Darius put an arm around Celia and they followed Ilya to the door, where he stopped and turned around. "I am a businessman, just as you said, Mister Minnich. However, if you double-cross me, or back out, I will force you to witness a tremendous amount of savagery visited upon your beautiful wife. And it will continue for days, until you give me what I want. If what you say is true, we will both become very rich and you will live out your days in Turkmenistan."

Opening the door, Ilya stepped out into the light of early dawn. Darius had no way of knowing how long it had been since the men had boarded his yacht and killed his crew, aside from what Ilya had just told him. He stumbled up two stone steps and through the door, realizing that he was both very hungry and thirsty.

Once outside, Darius looked around. The building they'd been held in was a very low structure, the floor a couple of feet below ground level. It was surrounded by scraggly low brush, with palm branches hanging haphazardly from the roof.

In the distance, Darius could hear the soft rush of waves breaking on a shoreline not far away. Ilya turned away from the sound of the surf and led them across a rock-strewn landscape. Trees and shrubs were bent and twisted by years of wind, none more than ten feet tall. Darius had no idea where they were. He'd never seen such a landscape.

Ilya led them along a little-used trail that sloped upward slightly. After less than a hundred yards, they reached a low cliff that dropped down to shallow, still water, which extended as far as the eye could see.

The cliff curved in both directions, creating a small cove. From the high vantage point, Darius saw that they were on a long and obviously very narrow island, which stretched away to the north for quite a distance.

In the center of the cove, an old boat sat at anchor. It was large, nearly as big as the *Obsession*, with a raised pilothouse. A two-story cabin below the pilothouse extended from near the stern to nearly amidships and an open deck forward of that. Huge truck tires hung from the railing as fenders, and a tarp stretched across the foredeck, probably to provide shade, Darius figured.

As they descended a narrow path down the twenty-foot-high cliff, Darius could see that the water was very shallow and the boat was in danger of being stranded if the tide was falling.

Ilya waded out into the water, leading the way. Celia stumbled, but Darius caught her, putting her arm around his shoulder to help her wade through the shallow water. She hadn't said anything since Oleg had threatened her with the chain saw. He thought she might be in shock from the ordeal.

When they reached the boat, Ilya began climbing up a rickety-looking ladder leaning against the hull. Darius had been wrong—the vessel was already resting on the bottom, the water barely reaching his waist. He waited until the man reached the top, a good ten feet above him, before urging Celia to climb.

Faltering at first, Celia finally figured out what Darius wanted her to do and climbed up the old wooden ladder. Darius waited until she was near the top before he started up. He doubted the ladder would hold them both.

"Welcome aboard, Missus Minnich," Ilya said, helping Celia over the low wooden railing at the top.

Darius hurried up the ladder, and once he was on the deck of the boat, he looked around. It was a fishing boat, old but sturdy looking. Under the covering tarp was a large sliding hatch forward with a large red equipment box between the hatch and the cabin. He assumed the hatch covered the boat's hold.

"Follow me," Ilya instructed.

Going aft, Ilya opened a door at the back of the cabins, and Darius followed him down several steps into a large room, a table and chairs taking up most of it.

At the table sat two men, who rose as Darius helped Celia down the steps. One of the men said something to Ilya in a language Darius didn't recognize. Ilya snapped back at him, apparently giving orders. Instantly, the two men busied themselves, getting plates and utensils from a cabinet and placing them in front of two adjacent chairs.

Waving a hand toward the table, Ilya said, "Please, have a seat. My men will prepare you food."

As Darius helped his wife into a chair, one of the men placed two bottles of water in front of them. Darius quickly removed the cap on one and started to move it to Celia's lips. He stopped halfway and looked at Ilya.

"You do not trust me?" Ilya asked. He took a mug from a hook and then took the bottle from Darius's hand. He poured a little water in the mug and drank it. Placing the mug on the table and handing the bottle back to Darius, he said, "We're partners now, Mister Minnich."

Darius held the bottle to Celia's mouth, and she tilted it up, drinking thirstily. "Drink slowly, dear," he cautioned her.

Picking up the other bottle, Darius twisted the cap off and took a couple of swallows, then sat down next to Celia as Ilya pulled a chair out on the opposite side of the table and sat down.

A moment later, one of the men placed a bowl of whole and sliced fruit on the table in front of them. "Eat," Ilya said. "There is fish as well. Left over from last night, but still good."

Celia needed no coaxing, taking a large mango slice from the bowl and wolfing it down. Darius picked up a banana and peeled it, also eating it quickly.

"After your hunger and thirst are sated, Oleg will show you to a cabin where you can rest. The tide is falling, and we cannot leave until late this evening at the earliest."

"Leave?" Darius asked. "For where?"

"Cuba. However, we will probably stay here for another day."

The other crewman placed reheated snapper fillets on the plates in front of Darius and Celia. They ate hungrily as Darius considered this new information. So far, he hadn't given Dobrovska anything. If they were taken to Cuba, he might never find a way to escape. Not that escape would be difficult, but getting off the island would be.

"Oleg," Ilya said after Darius and Celia had satisfied their appetites, "take Mister and Missus Minnich to the lower deck and show them to one of the empty crew cabins."

Minutes later, the door was closed behind them and Darius heard it lock. The cabin was small, barely the length of the bunk and only a few feet between the bunk and the aft wall. He waited until he heard Oleg's footsteps retreat down the gangway and then tried the door. It was deadbolted from the outside, needing a key to open it from inside.

"Do you have any idea how we can get away?" Celia asked.

Darius turned to his wife, looking into her eyes in the dim light coming through the small window of the cabin. "You're feeling better now?"

"Yes," she replied. "I've been pretending to be incoherent."

Putting his arms around her, he held her close to his chest and whispered, "We'll find a way out. If not, I'll give them what they want."

"I don't want to live in some foreign country, Darius."

"The alternative is not living," he replied, holding her at arm's length and looking into her eyes again.

Celia turned away and walked across the small cabin to the window. It was nailed shut, but even if it hadn't been, it looked to be too small for either of them to get through.

Darius moved around the cabin, looking for anything they might use for a weapon. The bed was built in and barely large enough for two people. The small hanging closet was empty, not even a rod for clothes to hang from. Lifting the mattress on the bunk, he found nothing under it. At least it was moderately clean and they could rest.

"Let's get some sleep," Darius suggested.

"Sleep?" Celia asked, obviously aggravated with her husband. "We're on a boat, being held against our will, you're talking about committing treason, our captors want to take us to Cuba, and you want to go to sleep?"

Taking her by the shoulders again, Darius said, "Celia, calm down. We've been through a lot. Neither of us is thinking clearly. There's no way out of here at the moment, and we're both beyond exhausted."

Sighing loudly, she turned and sat down on the edge of the bunk. "I'm sorry," she said. "You're right."

Gently, Darius pushed her back on the bunk and kissed her softly on the forehead before stretching out beside her. Within minutes, they were both sound asleep.

It seemed like only minutes had passed when Darius heard shouting from above. At first he had no idea where they were. As he sat up, full light was streaming in through the window. Rising from the bunk, he nearly lost his balance.

As Celia stood up, she was also confused and nearly fell, Darius catching her at the last moment. "What's going on?" she asked, a bewildered look on her face.

Looking out the window, Darius realized the boat was leaning several degrees. The tide had fallen completely, leaving the boat stranded on the sand and listing precariously. Below, he could clearly see the shadow of the boat on the wet sand, but the water had completely receded.

Celia said, "I hear something."

In the distance, Darius barely detected a low rumbling sound. It grew steadily louder, seeming to draw nearer, and then changed pitch to a deeper growl, growing fainter. The sound had at first seemed to have been coming from the north, but now appeared to be moving east and away from them.

Darius recognized it. "That's a plane!"

The shouting voices from above couldn't be made out, even if he could understand the language the men spoke. They were obviously excited, though. Leaning forward, he braced his hands against the hull on either side of the window and had to squat down to look up through the window toward the horizon. The boat was listing that much.

Celia joined him at the window, bending to look upward. The sound became fainter for a moment, then suddenly became louder again. "There!" she whispered urgently and pointed.

About a mile away, an antique-looking seaplane moved west across the island, no more than a hundred feet up. It then banked, turning sharply away from them.

"It's leaving," Celia said, frowning and dejected.

Listening for a moment, Darius whispered harshly, "No, it's turning."

As they listened, they could tell that the plane was getting closer, flying very low and slow. Darius didn't know anything about old seaplanes, but didn't think they would be very fast. It seemed to be following the opposite coast, where he'd heard the surf breaking earlier. The plane seemed to pass in front of the boat and then the engine sound diminished, lost in the dense wood of the boat's hull.

"I think they're looking for something," Celia said. "Could it be someone searching for us? Do you think they saw the boat?"

"I don't know," Darius replied. "They might be a part of Dobrovska's crew, looking for a place to land."

Once more, the pitch of the plane's engine changed. Darius knew by the sound that it was banking again, perhaps circling once more.

"Those men don't sound like it's someone they're expecting," Celia said softly.

As the plane seemed to circle across the island, to the south of where the boat lay, the voices from above quieted.

"It's leaving," Celia moaned.

Suddenly, the sound of the plane's engine changed, seeming to roar like a wounded lion at the same time that a loud crack came from above, followed quickly by another.

"That's a gun!" Darius urgently whispered.

The sound of the plane changed several more times as it moved out past the stern of the boat, invisible from the window in their cabin. Then it settled into a steady but diminishing buzz.

"Now it's leaving," Darius said. "And if these guys were shooting at it, they're definitely not friends of theirs."

"I hope nobody was hurt," Celia whispered as she sat back down on the edge of the bunk.

Darius sat next to her and took her hand in his. Kidnapped by God only knew who, she'd been beaten, starved, humiliated, and threatened with a chain saw, but Celia's concern was for a stranger. Gently, he lifted her hand and kissed the back of it.

# CHAPTER TWENTY

Once we arrived back at the *Rusty Anchor* and had *Island Hopper* out of the water, Parsons hurried toward the parking lot, where his two MPs waited. He'd been on his satellite phone almost constantly during the trip back, comparing notes with Binkowski and updating his superiors.

Leaving Kim to do the postflight, Deuce and I hurried after Parsons. Linda stayed behind to help Kim, and Waldrup and Meg went inside to use the phone to make arrangements at their hotels.

"The ransom note is a distraction," Parsons told me and Deuce as we caught up with him, just as he ended another phone call. "I'm sure of it."

"What did Binkowski come up with?" Deuce asked.

"Only six people working for the company know that the Minniches are missing. Miss Juarez, Captain Waldrup, the Minniches themselves, obviously, and two people in the accounting department. Waldrup was with me at the time the ransom note was dropped in the UPS box in Coconut Grove. Juarez was at the company office since yesterday morning. She never went home last night, and security protocols confirm it."

"And the two bean counters?" I asked.

"Binkowski is checking their alibis. Both left the office yesterday afternoon. Either of them could have made the drop."

"Which two in accounting?" Waldrup asked as he and Meg approached.

"Jack Stennis and Marjory Henderson," Parsons replied. "How's the leg?"

"Still intact," Waldrup replied. "I don't think the bullet did more than ding the titanium. Marjory is a problem."

"How so?" Deuce asked.

"Mister Minnich's first wife's maiden name was Henderson. Darlene Henderson Minnich. Her brother is Marjory's husband."

"You mean Minnich kept his ex-wife's sister-in-law on the payroll after the divorce?" Parsons asked, surprised.

The big man just shrugged. "She's good at her job. Besides, she despised Darlene."

Just then, Marty pulled into the parking lot in his pickup, climbed out, and walked to where we were standing. "Hey, Jesse. Where's Kim?"

"Checking the plane over with Linda," I replied. "Anything new from the forensics guys or Doc Fredric?"

"Nothing at all came back on the fingerprints. Still waiting on DNA. Doc Fredric confirms Meg's suspicion that the leg was cut off with a chain saw. He also confirmed the obvious COD of Mister and Missus Albright. Close-contact gunshot wound to the head."

Lifting his camera, Deuce said, "I need to use your computer, Jesse." Then he turned to Parsons and added, "You should join us. The equipment on the boat is a lot better than your phone."

Once we were aboard the *Revenge*, Deuce powered up the laptop, removed the memory card from the camera, and stuck it in a slot on the side of the computer. The memory card had over two hundred images, from the time we first saw the little building on South Anguilla until just after I took control of the plane from Kim. Connecting a UHB cable from the computer to the big-screen TV, Deuce displayed the images on the TV so we could all see.

Studying the photos of the small building, Deuce said, "Looks like either it's a very short structure or part of it is below ground."

"How can you tell that?" Meg asked. "There isn't anything to give you scale."

"See the sides, here?" Deuce said, getting up and pointing to the spot on the TV screen. "You can just make out the seams of the plywood walls. The sheets are square, so I'm guessing that the walls are only as high as these sheets are wide. Four feet."

"Do you think it belongs to the people on the boat?" Waldrup asked, looking at the TV screen.

"Most likely," Deuce replied. "Or at least used by them for something. It's the only building of any kind for miles, and that boat wasn't there by accident."

Sitting back down at the settee, Deuce skipped forward until he got to the frames of the boat itself. Parsons leaned in close. "Damn, it is a Nikonov AN94." Looking up at me, he said, "Sharp eye. Is there only that one hole in your plane?"

"Kim's checking her over now. Why?"

"Got a pretty clean image of the shooter," Deuce interrupted.

We all looked toward the big screen on the forward bulkhead of the salon again. The boat was obviously sitting high and dry on the wet sand, listing to port. Deuce zoomed in on the man leaning out of a starboard porthole on the forward part of the upper deck, just behind and below the pilothouse.

A shadow from the antenna mast partly covered his face. Deuce zoomed in more, framing just his face. Then he played with the contrast a little, taking out enough of the shadow to see his left eye. This left the other side of his face nearly whited out. I'd learned a little talking to Chyrel and knew that the clarity of the image wasn't as important as a full-frontal image showing both eyes. This allowed Chyrel's facial recognition software to make distance comparisons to the other features.

Cropping the image, Deuce connected to the email server and attached the picture to an email to Chyrel, in her office up in Homestead. Then he went back to flipping through the images.

"Why did you ask about a second hole?" I asked Parsons.

"When you first said the gas block was in front of the grip and it had a forward-curving magazine, I thought it might be the Nikonov, and that picture confirms it in my mind. It was designed to fire a two-round burst. With the gas block almost at the end of the barrel, there's almost no felt recoil from the first round before the second is fired, allowing the shooter to get two rounds on target."

"Is it accurate?"

Parsons grinned at me. "I checked up on you. You were a sniper instructor, huh? Probably nothing you'd be interested in. No more range than the AK, but just as accurate at a comparatively short range."

"Got a partial on the name of the boat," Deuce said. "Only part of the first word. Something ending with M-A, and then *Esperanza*."

I leaned in closer. There was a shirt dangling off the stern rail, covering most of the first word. "*Something Hope?*"

"*Última Esperanza?*" Waldrup suggested, staring at the image on the TV screen, his huge arms crossed over his chest. "Last Hope?"

Deuce was already preparing a second message to Chyrel, asking her to search vessel registries for possible names and owners. He cropped and attached that image as well. Then he clicked on the *Soft Jazz* icon on the desktop, opening the video conference icon.

A moment later, Chyrel's face appeared. "Hey, boss. I have facial recognition running, but it'll probably take a little while."

"How long until the bird will be over the location?" Deuce asked. He'd texted her the GPS position of the boat on the way home and instructed her to move the surveillance satellite to the position over the southern part of Cay Sal Bank.

"Several hours," she replied. "It'll be within range for an oblique view in about ninety minutes. What will I be looking for when it gets there?"

Deuce pulled up the best picture of the fishing boat and sent it to her. "This boat, and a small structure on the middle of the island immediately east of the boat."

"What if the boat moves?"

"It won't," Deuce replied. "At least, not anytime soon. It's high and dry. Can you pull up a tide chart for the southern Cay Sal Bank?"

She nodded, and within seconds another window opened. "There isn't an official one for that specific area," Chyrel said. "This is a four-day approximation based on other known areas nearby."

Looking up at me, Deuce asked, "Best guess on that boat's draft?"

I studied the picture again. There wasn't much to give it scale. But I figured the door to the pilothouse was probably six feet at least, and the distance from the wet sand to the boat's waterline looked to be a little more than half that.

"Shoal draft boat," I said. "At least three feet. Maybe four. They're not going anywhere until after sunset."

"I'll have eyes on them about then," Chyrel said. "But not directly overhead. ETA on that is nineteen thirty."

"That's cutting it pretty close," Parsons said, looking at the tide estimates. "Water'll be three feet above mean low tide before then."

"Yeah, but the skipper'd be a fool to try to move the boat before he has at least a foot of water under the keel," I said.

Pescador had been lying on the floor by the aft section of the couch and lifted his head, cocking an ear to the hatch. Just then, Kim, Marty, and Linda came into the salon.

Squatting down, Kim scratched Pescador's ears. "The *Hopper's* all secure, Dad."

I looked at her with a smile. "You didn't happen to find a second bullet hole, did you?"

"A second bullet hole? No. But then, I wasn't looking for one."

Linda stepped past us and into the galley. "Kim would have noticed it," she said, pouring a cup of coffee and sitting down next to me at the end of the settee. "She went over the whole plane with a fine-tooth comb."

"Shooting at an aircraft is a federal offense," Deuce said.

I knew where he was heading. "Yeah, but the Cay Sal Bank is part of the Bahamas, and last I heard, we had a pretty good relationship with them."

"What was the name of that Bahamian police sergeant?" Deuce asked.

"Cleary," I replied. "No good, though. Cay Sal Bank isn't in that district. It's part of the Bimini District."

"Maybe he knows someone there we can talk to?"

"I'll see if I can get in touch with him," I replied.

"Want his number?" Chyrel asked from the video feed.

Deuce grinned as he handed me his sat phone. "Yours is probably in the freezer."

Pulling my own phone from my pocket, I said, "Nope. What's the number, Chyrel?" She gave it to me and I punched it into my phone.

"You weren't kidding about having better resources," Parsons said to Deuce.

Cleary answered on the third ring. When I said who I was, he replied, "Please tell me you are not coming back to my island, Captain McDermitt."

I grinned. Cleary is a police sergeant on the island of Elbow Cay, in the northern Bahamas. We'd met when I went there, along with Deuce and a few others, to look for a lost Spanish treasure.

"No, Cleary. At least, not anytime soon."

"Den what can I do for you?"

I explained the situation, as much of it as I could, and how time was of the essence. He listened politely and finally said, "Yes, I know people in di Bimini District police. But dey will not give you permission."

"This boat's probably going to leave in less than five hours," I said, failing to disguise the rising anger.

"Bimini won't be able to send anyone dere until morning. You didn't hear me say dis, but if you leave now, you will be in and out long before dey can get dere, and nobody will know."

I grinned. Then Cleary said, "But, I must contact Bimini and tell dem dat a source told me dere was a problem out dere. Dey will send a boat, but it will be noon before dey get dere."

"Thanks, Cleary," I said. "Beer's on me next time I come to Elbow Cay."

I ended the call and turned to Deuce. "How fast can you get a few guys down here?"

Marty and Kim had sat down on the L-shaped couch, but she jumped to her feet, as did Linda. "Oh no," Kim said. "You're not going down there again."

"She's right," Linda added. "You're not going, are you?"

I looked from one to the other. Then I looked at Waldrup. I'd promised the big man that we'd get his cousin's killer. I turned to Deuce. "We'll take the Cigarette, with Rusty's Zodiac on board. Less than an hour to get there. How soon can you get an insertion team down here?"

Kim wheeled and stomped out of the salon, Pescador on her heels. "Kim, wait!" I shouted after her.

"I can have a four-man team here in less than an hour," Deuce said, already working on an email. "By the time you insert them, we'll have eyes on the boat." Pausing, he looked up at me. "Maybe you ought to at least think about staying on the boat."

I looked over at Linda. Being a cop, she knew the risk involved and it showed on her face. "I'm planning to," I replied.

"I'll go tell her," Linda said, the relief evident on her face.

Once she was gone, I said to Deuce, "As backup."

"Did you get the new tanks installed and hooked up?"

"Yeah," I replied. "The extra weight makes it a pig, but it'll still do better than ninety-five. It's only about a hundred and twenty miles, one way. With the extra tanks installed, it'll have a range of two hundred and fifty miles easy, at wide-open throttle. Double that at cruising speed."

Deuce sent the email. It went to four of his best operatives. Scott Grayson and Jeremiah Simpson were both former Marine Recon dive instructors. Andrew Bourke and Jeremy Dawson were former Coast Guard maritime enforcement specialists. Grayson, with his experience as a Recon Marine, would be in charge of the insertion team.

Kim and Linda came back in, Pescador leading the way. "You promise you'll stay on the boat?" Kim asked. I could see that she'd been on the verge of tears. This was still new territory for me. I'd been absent from her life nearly as long as she'd been alive. Though I care deeply for my two daughters, and have cared about others over the years, I couldn't recall anyone caring about me with this kind of fervor.

When she sat back down next to Marty, I went to her and knelt on one knee. "I can't promise that, kiddo. And I won't lie. I have every intention of inserting the guys and hanging back. I'm too old for this, and I've been trying to tell Deuce that for over a year." I looked back and he just grinned and shrugged.

Turning back to Kim, I looked deeply into her eyes. "I'm not gonna lie to you. If the insertion team needs help, I'm right there. The team Deuce is bringing down is top-notch. Andrew, Jeremy, Scott, and Jeremiah."

"Andrew and Scott?" she asked, a hopeful look on her face. "Good, they're both the opposite of you. Slow and methodical. And not likely to fly off the handle."

I gently pushed a strand of blond hair over her shoulder. "Yeah, they're that, alright. Besides," I said, looking up at Linda, "I have a lot of reasons to keep the axe head in place these days."

"How can we help?" Linda asked, placing a hand on my daughter's shoulder.

I took Kim's hands in mine and nodded to Marty, who had been sitting quietly next to her. "Think you and

Marty can go up to the island in his boat and bring the Cigarette down here?"

Kim thought it over. She knew my penchant for recklessness, but she also knew I wouldn't lie to her. "Sure," she replied. "It'll take less than an hour if we leave right now."

I looked back at Deuce and he nodded. "Andrew and Jeremy are just up in Islamorada, at Andrew's dive shop. They'll both be here within thirty minutes. Scott and Jeremiah are at Homestead and can be at Marathon Airport in less than an hour."

"Should I contact the sheriff?" Marty asked.

"Technically, the investigation is still in your hands, Marty," I said. "The federal government is only providing assets to the sheriff's office, and he hasn't removed you from the case, has he?" Marty shook his head. "But in this case, maybe you shouldn't say anything to him. We'll kinda be illegally entering a sovereign nation."

Nodding his understanding, he took Kim's hand, and the two went out the hatch. A moment later, I heard the outboard on his patrol boat start up and begin idling down the canal.

Turning, I said sarcastically to Deuce, "Speaking of informing your superiors, why haven't you *cleared this with the director?*"

He grinned mischievously, reminding me a lot of his dad. Russ was sometimes known to give his superiors only the intelligence they absolutely needed, and he'd often improvised in the field.

"*Technically,*" Deuce said, "I'm still the acting director until Monday morning."

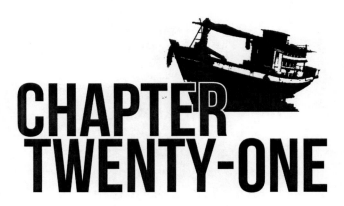

# CHAPTER TWENTY-ONE

Hearing footsteps approaching the door to the cabin, Celia clutched at her husband. There was a click from the lock, and the door flew open. Ilya Dobrovska stood in the hallway, a machine gun with a long, curved magazine hanging from a sling across his chest. "It is time to make good on the first part of our agreement, Mister Minnich."

"Who was in that plane?" Darius asked.

"I do not know," Ilya replied. "But they have fled and will not be returning. Please come with me. We have the computer set up in the galley and connected to the satellite."

As the two started to rise from the bunk, Ilya said, "Just you, Mister Minnich." Oleg stepped up behind Ilya. "Oleg will keep Missus Minnich occupied while we work. Be warned, if you hesitate, or I think you are trying to do something other than what we agreed on, that savagery I mentioned will commence immediately and you will be brought down here to witness it."

Turning to his wife, Darius said, "Wait here. I'm not going to do anything other than what he wants me to. You'll be alright."

Celia nodded slightly, then cast her gaze to the floor, her blond hair falling forward, hiding her face. She sat back down and quickly scooted back on the bunk as far into the corner as she could get, drawing her knees up to her chest and hugging them. Oleg stepped into the cabin, and Darius followed Ilya into the hallway. The door closed and Darius heard the click of the lock. Navigating the hallway was difficult with the deck pitched, but Darius did as Ilya did, pushing off the wall with his left hand.

"He won't touch her?" Darius asked.

"As per our agreement, Mister Minnich. The computer is set up directly above this cabin. He will not harm her unless I say to."

With Ilya following, Darius went up the steps at the end of the hall to the main deck. The same laptop as before was on the table and Darius sat down in front of it. Two leather-bound books wedged against each other and the opposite table rail kept the laptop from sliding.

"Can you hear me, Oleg?" Ilya asked in a normal tone, placing his gun against the cabinets on the far wall.

"Yes," came a somewhat muffled reply, but still quite clear. "I can hear you."

Sitting down across from Darius, Ilya tented his fingers and looked across the screen at Darius. "The laptop has a very large storage disk, which is nearly empty. All you have to do is download all the files dealing with the suit onto it and the first part of our transaction is complete."

It only took Darius a few minutes to gain access to his company's mainframe through the backdoor portal he'd created. A moment later, his finger hovered above the Enter key. "How do I know I can trust you?"

"You can't," Ilya replied matter-of-factly. "It is I who am trusting you, Mister Minnich. My clients do not understand security protocols, as I do. Your description of the disable coding makes perfect sense to me, and I trust that you will deliver it, once I've taken you to a place where you will be safe. If it is worth what you say, I will have no trouble at all in giving you half of what we make on the second part of our agreement."

Darius looked into the other man's eyes for a moment, then clicked the key to begin the download. Ilya came around the table and looked at the screen. A progress bar began to show the percentage of the documents that were downloading and displayed a completion time of just over three hours.

Checking his watch, Ilya said, "It should be completed by the time the tide has risen enough for us to leave here."

"For Cuba?" Darius asked, his face grim. Not that it mattered any longer. He'd already committed treason, though the American government wouldn't know about it for months.

Ilya grinned. "For only a short time, Mister Minnich. I have changed my mind about continuing to deal with the Cuban government. This transaction will make me very rich, and I will no longer need them to look the other way. Nor will I be giving them part of the profit. When we leave here on the evening tide, we will go to a

199

small town one hundred and twenty kilometers south of here on the Cuban mainland called Caibarién."

"And from there?"

Ilya shrugged. "My clients will meet us there. They have very good resources and will make Canadian passports for all of us, while their technicians examine what you have just given me. In two days, if the technicians say I have lived up to my end of the deal, I will be paid and we will fly to my home country."

Darius looked down at the computer screen. The progress bar ticked from two to three percent. Looking again at the man who had kidnapped him and his wife and most likely murdered his friends and crew, Darius said, "I don't think Celia will like Turkmenistan."

"With what I am going to pay you," Ilya said, with a grin, "you may live anywhere you choose. However, you should consider your new home's extradition treaty with the United States."

"You mean, we'll be free to go anywhere we want?"

Ilya stood. "Yes, anywhere you desire. It may take my clients several months to develop the suit and then have need of the particular line of coding you mentioned. Until then, you and your wife will be guests at my compound outside the capital, Ashgabat."

# CHAPTER
# TWENTY-TWO

S cott and Jeremiah arrived in Scott's van. He'd had his new dive shop's logo and name painted on the side of it. Scott climbed out and went to the back, taking two small duffle bags, before walking toward where Deuce, Parsons, and I stood waiting on the dock. Jeremiah then backed out and drove off. He'd wait for Andrew and Jeremy at the airport, where they would be arriving by helicopter.

"How's the dive business going?" I asked as the big black man dropped the bags by a hibiscus.

"Actually, better than I thought it would. We hired a few people and the shop's still open while we're gone."

"What'd you tell the employees?"

"Same thing we always do, Gunny," Scott replied, shaking my hand. "Told 'em we're goin' fishing. They seem to find it amusing that two black guys like diving and fishing. Actually, I suspect they think we're gay and just going to Key West for a weekend tryst."

Laughing with him, I introduced Scott to Parsons and then Waldrup and Meg as they came out of the *Revenge*. Deuce explained the plan we'd come up with to Scott, bringing him up to speed. He asked a few questions about details, but mostly nodded, absorbing what Deuce was telling him. He'd learned to respect and trust Deuce's decisions and intuition.

The unmistakable sound of the Cigarette's twin eleven-hundred-horse racing engines could be heard long before we saw it. The scream of those engines carries a long way, and from the sound, Kim was nearly at full throttle. The boat suddenly appeared as it rounded Sister Rock before slowing down for the entry to Rusty's canal.

The sound of the big, throaty racing engines idling into the canal brought Rusty out. "I ain't even gonna ask," he said as he stood beside me, watching Scott help Kim tie the boat up.

"Probably for the best," I agreed. "Mind if I borrow your Zodiac and the muffled engine?"

"I'll get it and put it in the cabin, along with a couple of air tanks to fill it from and enough gas to get you thirty miles," Rusty replied as Scott approached.

Even if Rusty hadn't known anything about Deuce and his team or about my involvement with them, his answer would have been the same. We'd shared so much over the years, he was literally the brother I'd never had. We each knew that the other would do or provide anything without hesitation, even step in front of a bullet if need be.

"You remember Scott?" I asked Rusty. Though they barely knew one another, they had a bond almost as strong. The two shook hands and grunted an *oohrah*, as Marines are apt to do.

Scott loaded his and Jeremiah's bags aboard, and Rusty took Scott toward the boat shed at the end of the dock. Jeremiah was already filling the auxiliary tanks on the go-fast boat, so Kim and I left Deuce and Parsons and went aboard the *Revenge*.

"You want me to get your fly rod case?" Kim asked hesitantly.

I considered it a minute. The M40 in the case she mentioned is a great rifle, but it needs a really stable platform. "No, there's two shorter cases next to it," I replied. "Grab one of those and one of my Sigs with two extra magazines."

A moment later, she returned with the case and placed it on the counter. Nobody has yet said anything to me directly about it, but I've heard there are people that would disapprove of a father exposing his child to firearms. Personally, I think those people are idiots. A parent can't expect to hover over their children like a drone, always there to protect them. Kim has become a very good marksman over the last year, and she's been taught the correct way to handle firearms. I limit her exposure to dangerous situations, as much as a father can. But, if trouble comes, she's got the ability and training to meet it head-on.

Hearing tires crunching on the crushed-shell drive outside, I looked and saw Jeremiah pulling back into the lot. I went down to my stateroom and changed quickly into black cargo pants and a black long-sleeved shirt. Then I grabbed two boxes of 5.56mm ammo for the Tavor bullpup as well as a box of 9mm cartridges for the Sig.

Returning to the salon with my go bag, I found Linda and Kim were both busy in the galley, making sandwiches for us to take with us. Meg and Waldrup were sitting on the couch to the stern, talking quietly. I opened the case and took out the Israeli TAR-21 bullpup machine gun, checked that it was empty, and placed it into my go bag.

As I began loading the four magazines that were in the case, Waldrup rose and came across the salon. "That boat has six seats," he said.

I looked up at the man. I knew exactly what he meant. His employer and his wife had been taken, and he was their head of security. He was also an Airborne Ranger, which further strengthened his loyalty.

"Not my call, Miguel," I said quietly while loading the mags. "You'll have to clear it with Deuce."

"What kind of man is he?" Waldrup asked, quietly.

Placing two loaded magazines in the go bag, I thought about the question for only a second. "Probably the most capable and honorable man I've ever met. And a crazy good judge of men. I wouldn't be surprised if, after this is over, he doesn't start trying to recruit you. But, going along on an illegal insertion to rescue hostages? I don't know. Just be straight up and ask him. Maybe you can stay with me on the boat as ready reserve."

Waldrup left then and I went back to loading magazines, noting that Meg followed Waldrup outside. After finishing the last two of the Tavor's magazines, I started loading the two 9mm mags for my Sig and then put them all in the go bag as well.

"Will this be enough?" Kim asked. They'd filled a small cooler with enough sandwiches to feed a small army and a second one with at least a dozen bottles of water.

I grinned at my youngest. "What're the other guys gonna eat?"

Kim punched me in the shoulder, grinning. Then she and Linda followed me outside. Deuce and Waldrup were standing up by the bow of the Cigarette in what looked like a deep conversation. Deuce appeared to be doing most of the talking. Stepping down into the rear cockpit, I went forward and stowed my gear in the small, now completely stripped, cabin.

Originally, it had been nicely appointed with a small settee, a refrigerator, and a tiny private head forward. To offset the weight of the new auxiliary tanks, I had stripped it to the bare hull, leaving only the marine head and a small holding tank.

"Not quite so pretty in there anymore," Scott said as I stepped back up into the cockpit.

"Extra weight," I replied, starting the engines. "Don't need it."

Scott and I joined the others on the dock, as Andrew and Jeremy casually walked up, as if they were about to go for a sunset cruise. We shook hands all around and I introduced the two men to Parsons and Meg. Marty still hadn't made it back yet, but considering the disparity in the speed of his boat and the Cigarette, I didn't expect him.

"Good to see you again," Andrew said, his big baritone voice punctuating his words. "You're looking a lot fitter than last time I saw you."

"Linda's been keeping me in line," I said, glancing over to where Deuce and Waldrup appeared to be finishing up their mostly one-sided conversation. "Looks like we're about ready to shove off."

"Gentlemen," Deuce said, as he and Waldrup approached. "This is retired Army Captain Miguel Waldrup, formerly with the 101st Airborne and then with the 75th Rangers in Kuwait. With Jesse's permission, he's going to go along as part of the backup with Jesse."

I grinned at the big man. "Welcome aboard, Captain."

While the other team members shook hands with Waldrup, I turned to Kim. "Would you mind bringing me that other case and another box of five-point-five-sixes?"

As Kim disappeared into the *Revenge*, Deuce stepped over and pulled me aside. "He has his own sidearm, and I deputized him."

"You can do that?"

"At least until Monday morning," Deuce replied, grinning like his dad once again. "He's to be *your* backup, Jesse. He's not to get off the boat for any reason. Think he can borrow something a little more useful?"

I nodded toward Kim, stepping over the *Revenge's* gunwale, carrying the other, shorter fly rod case. A few onlookers were down the dock, watching. I recognized all of them as liveaboards.

"Miguel," I called over to the group. "Take that fly rod case from Kim and put it down in the cabin. It's yours for a while. Open it and rig the tackle while you're down there."

Quickly disappearing through the tiny hatch, I had a mental image of him trying to move around in the low, cramped space. I had to bend over to keep from banging my head, and he was nearly as tall as me, but much bigger everywhere else.

"Scott, Jeremy, get the lines," I shouted and turned to Linda and Kim. "We'll be back before twenty-one hundred," I said, taking Linda in my arms and holding her close for a moment. Then I stepped back and pulled Kim into the hug. "Don't worry. We'll all be fine."

Waldrup came up out of the cabin, grinning. He easily vaulted the gunwale and went over to where Meg stood in the shade of a royal palm. They seemed to be having an intimate conversation, which surprised me. They'd only known each other a day.

Finally, Marty's patrol boat idled up the canal. He quickly tied off and came over to where we were standing. "Glad I got here before you left," he said. "That thing is fast!"

"If you want," I said to Marty, "you can stay aboard till we get back. We have encrypted communication, and you can keep track of what's going on."

"Thanks, Jesse," Marty replied. "I will."

"We'll be back by twenty-one hundred," I told him firmly.

He grinned at Kim. "Yes, sir. I know. Rules eight and ten."

Slapping him on the shoulder, I stepped over the gunwale and got settled in the first seat and Andrew took the second seat to my left. Waldrup was forced to the port side, since the two outboard seats had a couple of extra inches of shoulder room.

Each of Deuce's team members carried redundancies for just about everything. I knew before we left the canal, one of them would give Waldrup an earwig. He was dressed in blue jeans and a dark brown long-sleeved shirt. The team didn't usually carry extra clothes, and even if they did, nothing they'd have would fit the guy. So, he was as covert as he was going to get.

Rusty shoved the bow away from the dock as Deuce pushed the stern out. I put the starboard engine in forward and the port engine in reverse, spinning the forty-two-foot racing boat and pointing it toward the end of the canal. Then I put the port engine in forward and we idled toward open water, the growling engines seeming to anticipate the fast crossing of the Gulf Stream to come.

I knew none of the people watching from the dock were fooled for a second. Six men, like we had aboard, don't go fishing in a Cigarette boat. Rusty would come up with some kind of story that would appease anyone who asked. But, here in the Keys, people mostly don't bother asking. We've seen it all before.

Reaching the small jetty at the end of the canal, I eased the throttles forward slowly. The sonar unit wasn't as good as the one on the *Revenge*—it wasn't directional, but it showed me that we had six feet under us. Enough depth for most boats with an equal draft to throttle up and get on plane. But the sheer power of these engines could displace a lot of the water very fast and swamp the stern as the props dug into the sandy bottom.

Digging in my cargo pocket, I took the tiny box with the earwig out. Opening it, I turned on the device and put it in my ear, adjusting the springy mic around my ear so that it was in contact with my upper jawbone.

"Alpha Two. Comm check," I said in a normal tone as I took my Pulsar Edge night vision goggles out of my go bag, which was secured next to my seat. It was still more than thirty minutes until sunset, but once underway, I didn't want to have to fumble with it.

"Alpha One," Deuce's voice said, sounding as if he were whispering in my ear.

"Alpha Three," Andrew chimed in. One by one, the four men in back reported, Waldrup last.

"Good luck, Alpha Team," came a familiar voice.

"Didn't know you'd be joining the party, Colonel," I said.

"You should know by now, Jesse. I'm with you guys in one way or another every time you go out."

Deuce's voice came over the earwig. "Alpha Seven, meet *my* boss, Colonel Travis Stockwell."

"You be careful, son," the colonel said. "You're strictly backup out there. Hooah?"

"Hooah, sir," Waldrup replied, grinning.

Easing both throttles a bit further, the go-fast slowly came up on plane. I pointed the bow southeast, toward Dog Rocks at the northeast corner of Cay Sal Bank, and slowly inched the throttles further.

I kept the speed under seventy knots until we cleared the reef line, then pushed the throttles to the stops. As the boat rocketed forward, the powerful racing engines screamed like banshees and pressed us all into our seats.

"Holy shit!" I heard Waldrup say, followed by a couple of muted laughs. "I thought we were already going full speed."

# CHAPTER TWENTY-THREE

The crossing to Dog Rocks only took forty-five minutes, the sun disappearing before we got there. Andrew spent nearly all of that time concentrating on the gauges on his side and feeding me updates in a calm voice. I had matching gauges for oil pressure, oil temperature, and water temperature on my side. But at a hundred knots, if you take your eyes off the water for even half a second, the boat will travel a good eighty-five feet. In the dark, even with night vision, a glance at the gauges would take a lot longer than that.

Turning south at the edge of the bank, we began taking the small rollers on the port beam, so I slowed to eighty knots. As we knifed through the inky darkness, the night vision goggles turned everything to a gray-green, which didn't really give any clue as to water color, a good indicator of depth. I stayed half a mile off the nearly straight line that bounded the bank, knowing we had very deep water out here.

There'd been the usual conversation among the men in back. The same typical questions military men and women ask one another when they meet. The team felt Waldrup out to determine where he'd been, what action he'd seen, and what his skills were. Waldrup in turn asked a few questions about the team. But as we neared the spot where we planned to transfer the insertion team to the Zodiac, talk ceased. All the men donned their own night vision goggles and began going over their gear once more.

Ten minutes later, I could see the surf breaking on Bellows Cay and turned toward it. From there it was about eight miles to South Anguilla Cay. I slowly brought the speed down, and just a couple hundred yards from the tiny island, we came down off plane and I shifted the engines to neutral and shut them off. There was no chance that the throaty rumble of the big engines could be heard this far away from the Anguillas.

Within a few minutes, without any conversation, Andrew and Jeremy had the Zodiac inflated, the motor mounted to the transom, and the gas tanks aboard. Andrew started the forty-horse muffled Mercury engine, the sound of water spraying from the piss tube making more noise than the engine exhaust.

A moment later, the other three men transferred their equipment and climbed over into the inflatable boat. It was more than large enough for twice as many people, so they had plenty of room. With Jeremy in the bow as lookout and Scott and Jeremiah taking up spots on either side behind him, they shoved off and Andrew had the little boat up on plane, moving almost soundlessly away to the south.

Waldrup took the second seat and I started the engines. "Feel around in my bag," I said. "There's a Night Spirit monocular in there."

He found it and turned it on. Standing, he braced his hip against the side of the boat and steadied himself against the light chop with his left hand on the low windshield. Raising the small scope to his eye, he scanned the area in the direction the Zodiac had disappeared. "What is it you want me to tell you?"

"Just locate and keep an eye on our guys," I replied. "Alpha One, do you have eyes on the target yet?"

"Not yet," Deuce responded. "That cove they were anchored in shelters them from oblique view. The bird's nearly overhead, though."

"Are you sure you gave me the right coordinates, boss?" I heard Chyrel ask in the background. "'Cause I'm not seeing anything down there."

Putting the engines in gear, I gave the boat just enough throttle to get up on plane. At only twenty-five knots, the responsiveness of the big racing boat was sluggish at best, as it wallowed in troughs between the small rollers, stern down and bow high in the air.

The insertion team was heading to a spot on the lee side of the island a little north of where we'd seen the shack. They would go ashore there, and I'd power up and go screaming around the southern tip of the island as a diversion. This would allow the team to move faster across the island, secure the building, and then move to the west side and take the boat.

"Found 'em," Waldrup said. "They just passed the end of this island here and are turning away from us."

"Keep a close eye on them," I said. "Let me know when they disappear on the west of the Anguilla bunch."

Knowing this particular island only slightly, all I could really recall is that it had a pretty high profile compared to the other islands that made up Cay Sal Bank. The windward side is mostly undercut cliffs, four to six feet high, with few places to land or go ashore. The center is probably ten feet above the high tide. The target boat was pretty low profile, even with its higher rear decks. Tucked deep inside that little cove on the western side, Chyrel might not be able to see it until the satellite gets almost directly above.

"When you're feet dry, Alpha Three," Deuce said, reading my thoughts as he so often does, "get small and wait until we have eyes on the target from above."

"Roger that," Andrew replied.

We continued at a very slow twenty-five knots for the next few minutes, the engines burbling just above an idle. Keeping pace with the Zodiac, which was now running inside the edge of the bank in just ten feet of water, we paralleled their course. Though less than half a mile from them, we were in over three hundred feet of water.

"They disappeared behind the first of the islands," Waldrup said, sitting back down.

"I can see both of you," Deuce said. "Alpha Two, you're gonna have to just hang out offshore until we have eyes on the target."

"Roger that," I said, slowly bringing the go-fast boat down off plane, then shifting to neutral and killing the engines.

I felt pretty confident that anyone on the boat or island, which were now only a few miles away, wouldn't have heard the sound of our engine while we were bare-ly idling along. Removing the starlight goggles, I waited until my eyes adjusted, then took the thermos from my go bag and filled a mug.

"Want some?" I asked the big man sitting next to me.

"Sure," he replied and I handed him the mug, pour-ing more into the screw-on cup for myself. "Waiting's never been one of my strong suits."

"You can't hurry time," I said. Then, because I knew Deuce and the others were listening, I added, "We're just taking a coffee break out here, Alpha One. Let me know when you have eyes."

"Be advised, Alpha Two," Deuce said. "Binkowski has taken Darlene Minnich into custody. Both her broth-er and sister-in-law are cooperating fully, but she's law-yered up."

"Marjory's fired, at the very least," Waldrup mut-tered.

"Don't rush to judgment," Deuce said. "It might have been just pillow talk, then the brother innocently told his sister, because she and your boss used to have a rela-tionship."

"A violation of both OpSec and PerSec on her part, sir," Waldrup replied, standing and looking toward the far island through the monocular. He leaned forward over the dash, as if trying to see over the island that sepa-rated him from the people that might have abducted his employers.

He was right, but he was also a military man, em-ployed by a civilian company as head of security. I fig-ured he'd probably written both the operational security and personal security doctrines for the company himself.

"More information coming in," Deuce said. "The boat's a Cuban-flagged fishing boat, home port of Guadiana Bay."

*Guadiana Bay*, I thought. *Popular place for bad people.* And the only place in Cuba where I've actually set foot on shore. "What else is there?" I asked.

"Internal National Revolutionary Police Force communications indicate the crew was surprised at the dock just before putting to sea almost a month ago. A gang of seven Caucasian attackers used automatic weapons to execute the crew members in front of onlookers. One of the attackers then used a chain saw to mutilate the bodies in full view of other people on the dock, as a threat to keep quiet."

"Apparently, at least one ballsy person didn't take the threat sitting down," I said.

"The most recent email is from the Minister of the Interior himself," Deuce said. "Ordering the local police to not pursue the case further."

"Black marketers and politicians," I muttered. "In bed with each other for the almighty dollar. A few poor fishermen's lives don't count for shit to these people." There was silence for several minutes, each member of the team weighing the information Deuce had just given us.

Some folks say that money is the root of all evil. I've even heard Bible-thumpers shouting it from soapboxes. It's not true, though. Money can be used for good. My grandfather taught me this when I was very young. I was raised by my dad's parents from the age of eight. Pap and Mam were wealthy by most standards, and Pap gave a lot of his earnings to his church and his charities. He showed me by example how good it felt to give and help others. It's the love of money, greed, which is usually at the center of bad things happening to good people.

Pap also taught me that I wasn't to stand idly by when someone was being hurt or bullied. Pap was a Marine like me and Dad. He'd fought in World War II and Dad was killed in Vietnam. Both men took up arms when good people were being threatened by bad. As had I.

"I'm feeling like an impatient buzzard, Colonel," I said, knowing that Travis was still listening in.

A moment later, Travis's voice came back. "Alpha One, go comm Zulu."

There was a slight buzz over the earwig, then Travis said, "I agree, Jesse. It's just me, Deuce, and you guys out there listening now. As of now, Alpha Team is weapons-free. You are clear to engage targets on sight. I repeat, no warnings and no waiting for them to shoot first. Does everyone understand? Sound off."

One by one, each of us acknowledged that we understood the change in our rules of engagement. This was a whole new game now. It's what most of the team members had joined up for. Not that they enjoyed killing indiscriminately, but the ROE on the battlefield leaves the warrior at a severe disadvantage that could cost him his life. When Waldrup agreed, Travis said, "Chyrel, you can bring the two listeners back online now."

*Two listeners*, I wondered. Then it dawned on me. Plausible deniability. Travis has only two people above him: the secretary of DHS and his boss, the president. Our communications were being monitored in the situation room of the White House, possibly even by the president himself. By shutting them out of the change in the ROE, Travis had taken full responsibility and given whoever the listeners were a way to say they honestly knew nothing about it.

As we drifted, I listened as Andrew reported that they'd made landfall and Scott was taking over the lead. Little was said as the men leapfrogged one another until they had a fifty-foot perimeter set up around the spot where they brought the Zodiac ashore. Then they hunkered down to wait for the satellite.

The wait wasn't very long.

# CHAPTER TWENTY-FOUR

The whirring sound of an electric motor woke Darius. He didn't know how long he'd been asleep, but it was dark outside, several bright stars visible through the window.

Earlier, as the files were downloading, one of Ilya's men made sandwiches, putting them and several bottles of water in a small cooler. Darius had then been allowed to return to the cabin without an escort. Oleg met him at the door, and once Darius was inside, Oleg locked the door and left.

Darius and Celia had eaten in silence, then stretched out to rest. That was in the early afternoon, so Darius knew they must have slept for several hours, at least.

"What's that noise?" Celia whispered, lying next to him on the small bunk.

"I don't know," Darius replied, rising from the bunk. "But the boat's no longer in danger of rolling over."

Listening, Darius could hear people talking outside. The whining noise was joined by the sound of an engine starting and then a loud clanking.

"They're hoisting anchor," Celia said. "We're leaving."

"For Cuba," Darius said. "The download must have finished."

"You shouldn't have agreed."

"We had no choice. They were going to kill me and sell you as a sex slave."

"I'd have fought them every step and they'd have had to kill me too," Celia said, resolutely.

"I couldn't let that happen. Besides, from what Ilya said, we might come out richer than we would have selling the suit to our own military."

In the faint light of the moon filtering through the window, Darius saw his wife look at him with an expression he'd never seen her display. Not quite revulsion, but something close to it.

"Better a dead patriot than a live traitor," she muttered.

"How can you say that?" Darius asked, crossing to the window and looking out. "We're alive. And soon, we'll have enough money to live very comfortably in some Third World country without an extradition treaty."

Celia joined her husband at the window. "I don't want to live in some cesspool of a country. And I don't want to be rich if it means what we do might cost American lives."

Turning to her, Darius looked into her eyes by the light of the moon. There was a hardness there he'd never noticed before.

"They don't have the disable code," he said softly. "It'll be months at least before they even know they need it. That buys us some time. Maybe we can find some way to get away before then. But, if it means us staying alive, I'm going to give it to them."

A grinding noise emanated from behind the cabin they were in. The boat lurched suddenly, and Celia stumbled into Darius's arms. As they looked out the window, they could see that the boat was slowly starting to move.

Celia had seen the change in her husband over the last few years, especially this past year. All his decisions and actions lately had been financially motivated, where before he'd been a staunch supporter of the military and his only concern had been manufacturing things that would better protect them on the battlefield.

"How far is it to Cuba?" Celia asked, turning away.

"I don't even know where we are. But if I had to guess, I'd say this island is part of that group of islands between the Florida Keys and Cuba. Anywhere from twenty to fifty miles."

"It doesn't look like a very fast boat."

"No," Darius replied. "We probably won't get there until daylight. Ilya said we would go to a town called Caibarién, a hundred and twenty kilometers from here, but I don't know how far that is."

"It's seventy-five miles," Celia replied, getting a curious look from her husband. She shrugged. "The distance of three marathons."

"Of course," Darius said. "All that running you do. No sooner than sunrise, then. I don't see this boat going more than ten miles an hour."

"It's only eighty-some miles from Key West to Havana," Celia said. "Could this be one of the islands in the Keys?"

"I think this Caibarién is further east, along the Cuban coast."

Outside the cabin, they each heard the sound of footsteps and turned toward the cabin door. The lock clicked and one of Ilya's crewmen swung the door open.

"Ilya say you are free to move around on boat," the man said in thickly accented English. "Food is in one hour." Darius led the way, stepping out into the hallway with the man. "The ladder is forward," the man grunted, pointing. "I go aft for sleep."

He left them standing in the hallway then. "Should we try to get up to the deck and jump?" Celia whispered.

"No," Darius replied. "They would just turn around and pick us up. We'll have to wait. Maybe when it gets later we can steal a dinghy or something."

Having no other options, they went up the ladder to the kitchen area, which was empty. Through the windows, they could look down on the side decks, where several men were working. More than Darius had originally thought were aboard.

"Up here," they heard Ilya say and turned toward the sound of his voice. They climbed the short ladder to the pilothouse, which afforded a view of the whole working deck below. "Dinner will be shortly. We need all hands to watch as we exit the cove."

A man up in the bow pointed and started waving anxiously, yelling something in their language. Ilya calmly spun the wheel and pushed on the throttle for a moment. The heavy boat responded sluggishly.

"How far are we from Cuba?" Darius asked point-blank.

"In a direct line?" Ilya said. "About sixty kilometers. To Cuban waters, about forty. But, where we are going is further east along the shore. We'll sail due south until we're inside Cuban waters and arrive in Caibarién several hours after sunrise."

The lookout on the bow signaled again, and Ilya spun the wheel in the opposite direction. A moment later, the man in the bow turned and waved both arms, then started walking aft. The boat was equipped with a cheap depth finder, like bass boats use, and Darius could see that they were in deep water, which was getting deeper very fast.

As the boat rounded the tip of the island, Darius could just make out the sound of another boat. It was very faint and sounded like one of those powerful racing boats. Probably way too far away to see the boat they were on, though. Knowing how well sound carried over water, he estimated the boat was a good five to ten miles distant and seemed to be slowing, the sound growing fainter.

If Ilya had heard the other boat, he didn't let on.

# CHAPTER TWENTY-FIVE

After drifting in mostly silence for twenty minutes, Deuce's voice came over my earwig. "Alpha Two and Three, the boat is not in the cove."

Waldrup stood quickly, bringing the monocular to his eye again. "The boat's gone?"

"We'll find it," Deuce said. "Zooming out and switching to thermal."

It was at moments like this that Deuce's natural calm and methodical leadership skills really shone through. I'd seen him operate in a few other dicey situations and was impressed with how he maintained a cool head—a trait he'd inherited from his father.

I waited patiently, drifting in the darkness, but realized I was holding my breath with my hand on the starters. Slowly, I released the air from my lungs as Waldrup sat down. A calm fell over the man, as it did me. For him, it was perhaps the result of his training. For me, it was a mixture of my own training, and my confidence in Deuce and the others in the team.

"Got him," Deuce finally said. "Five nautical miles due south and traveling south at seven knots."

"That's getting really close to Cuban waters," I reminded him.

"Twenty-five miles from the coast," Deuce replied.

At seven knots, the target would be inside Cuban waters in about two hours. At full throttle, I knew we could be on top of them in just a few minutes. We all waited for Deuce's plan.

"Alpha Three, head for the structure and investigate," Deuce ordered. "I see no heat signatures on the island at all. Alpha Two, swing inside and be ready to pick them up in the cove. The latest nautical charts show no shallow obstructions and eight to ten feet of water at high tide, which was thirty minutes ago."

"Roger that," I said, starting the engines. I engaged the transmissions, and we were up on plane in seconds, turning toward the wide gap between Bellows and Anguilla Cays. The Cigarette quickly accelerated and I turned south on the lee side of the Anguillas at seventy knots, hoping that Deuce's nautical charts were really new.

Scott and his team made it to the small shack we'd seen in just a few minutes. "Alpha One, the building is secure, nobody around. We did find signs that someone has been here recently, though. Several zip ties, which appear to have been cut, lying on the ground in two different spots. Plus, a few pearl buttons scattered at one of those spots."

"Head west to the cove," Deuce replied.

A few minutes later, I slowly brought the go-fast boat down off plane and idled into the cove where the target boat had once lain hidden from view.

Watching the depth finder closely, I brought the Cigarette to a stop in four feet of water, the insertion team already wading out to us. As each man neared the gunwale, Waldrup simply reached down and lifted them out of the water and they scrambled over the gunwale.

"Insertion team is aboard," I said as Andrew sat down in the second seat.

"Head due south," Deuce said. "We might be able to board from behind."

I thought about the pictures Deuce had taken. He was right—the stern of the *Última Esperanza* was low, and with the Cigarette matching its speed, our bow would be high. Looking over the windshield at the foredeck, it looked really narrow.

Tapping Andrew on the shoulder, I pointed ahead to the foredeck. "The only handholds are the two cleats about five feet back from the bow." Andrew stood and looked where I was pointing, while I tried not to hit anything leaving the cove.

Once in deeper water, I sat down and slowly brought the boat up on plane. When Andrew sat back down, I yelled, "Hang on."

Then I shoved the throttles to the stops and the powerful engines launched us like a rocket. Reaching eighty knots in just a few seconds, I brought the throttles back a little to reduce noise.

"It might work," Andrew said. He turned in his seat and discussed his idea with the others.

"Three miles ahead and closing fast," Deuce said. "They're still ten miles from Cuban waters. When you're within sight, slow down and visually recon the situation, then we'll decide. Thermal imaging shows the engine as a large hot spot on the stern, so anyone there is lost in it. Looks like three or four people in the pilothouse and three more up on the foredeck."

Within minutes, I could see the boat about a mile ahead and began to slow down. The Cigarette dropped off plane, settling in the water and riding bow high. Both Andrew and I had to stand to see over it as we idled along at ten knots.

Through the night vision, the rear of the boat was awash in light from inside the cabin. I could clearly see into what looked like the galley. It appeared to be vacant, as was the aft deck area.

"I don't see anyone at the stern," Andrew said. "It'll be a little different than how we've trained, but I think it'll work."

"Alpha One, keep a close eye on the three tangoes up on the foredeck," I said, nudging the throttles a bit. "Let me know if anyone moves aft."

At thirteen knots, we were going nearly twice as fast as *Última Esperanza* and gaining quickly. When we were within four hundred yards, the bow of the Cigarette was nearly blocking my view of the fishing boat and I slowed to just ten knots.

Andrew stood and slung his MP-5 on his back so that he could bring it forward quickly. Then, stepping up onto his seat, he went up and over the windshield. Jeremy took his place by the second seat as Andrew carefully moved forward on the deck, finally dropping onto all fours and crawling the last few feet.

Once Andrew was lying spread-eagle on the bow, holding a cleat in each hand, Jeremy followed and took up a position behind him, holding both ankles, his legs extended straight back, forming a cross.

Scott and Jeremiah followed right behind, each taking a spot on either side of Jeremy's legs. They grasped one another's forearms over the back of Jeremy's knees and locked their inboard ankles together. Their outboard hands gripped the rails, as did the toes of their outboard boots. This effectively locked all four men into position on the narrow foredeck. It was about as secure as they could be, in case we had to take evasive action.

Slowly, I put a little forward pressure on the throttles, and the sound of the burbling engines ticked up a notch. Waldrup came up to stand in front of the second seat, training the monocular on the stern deck of the boat ahead, his Tavor at the ready.

"No movement," Waldrup said.

"Forty meters," Deuce said. "Rate of closure is one meter per second."

I remembered the pilothouse had portholes in back, but this close, the long roof of the cabin would block anyone from seeing us. I hoped. I did a slow count to thirty in my head, then put a little back pressure on the throttles, slowing the boat just a hair. I could no longer see most of the fishing boat, our bow blocking the view.

"Come left for a second, then back to the right," Andrew instructed.

I barely moved the wheel, held it for a second, and turned it back the other way for another second before bringing it back to center.

"Perfect," Andrew said. "You're lined up with the left side of the stern. She's a single-screw."

I'd been hoping it was a twin-engine. A single dome of water pushed by one big prop is harder to ride up on. I guess Andrew had chosen the port side to allow me to see our approach better. Still, all I could see of the boat ahead was the starboard rail, so I was completely relying on Deuce and Andrew to bring us close enough that the men could jump down to the aft cockpit of the fishing boat.

"Ten meters," Deuce said, and I put a little more pressure on the throttles. "Alpha Three, go at one meter."

He started a count from five meters as I slowed the Cigarette just a bit more. On the foredeck, Scott and Jeremiah cocked their outboard legs a little, preparing to stand and charge forward.

We'd practiced this a few times, but boarding a variety of boats from the *Revenge*, with its handrails and high pulpit. We had actually taken down a boat this way once. But the narrowness of the Cigarette's foredeck made this maneuver a bit different.

Falling overboard at eight knots was unlikely to cause injury, but the delay in picking a man up might allow the *Esperanza* to make it to Cuban waters, which would open up a whole new set of problems. Not the least of which would involve patrol boats and MiG fighters.

Just as Deuce said two meters and Andrew began to stand up, two shots rang out, followed closely by two more.

"Hang on," I shouted, turning the wheel hard to starboard and dropping the throttles to an idle. When I felt the thrust from the other boat's prop begin to push the bow sideways, I jammed the throttles. The engines roared and I spun the wheel back to the left, hoping we were clear of the big boat. The props caught and the boat launched up onto plane instantly.

Next to me, Waldrup fired two successive short bursts from the MP-5, and when I looked back, I could see a man hanging limp out of one of the lower portholes, near the stern. Waldrup must have hit something else of importance too, because there was smoke coming from the stern.

"So much for a covert boarding," Andrew said, still hanging onto the bow cleats. "You wanna slow this thing down, so we can get up?"

We were a half mile from the other boat and had no lights on. There was no chance they could hit us from a moving boat, even with a night vision-scoped rifle. I slowly brought the Cigarette down to an idle, and the four men on the foredeck scrambled back to their seats.

"Someone shot at us, Deuce!" I said, dropping any pretense at covert communication. Not that it mattered. Our comm was encrypted, and Chyrel had once told me that even during training ops, she switched the whole team's frequency every few minutes.

"Sorry, Alpha Team," Deuce calmly said. "He must have been blotted out by the heat signature of the engine."

"What now, Alpha One?" I asked. "We returned fire, and the target appears to be dead in the water. One tango down."

"Wanna try hailing them and asking if they need help?" Jeremiah suggested. Usually a very quiet and introspective man, his comment brought a chuckle from me and Scott.

"What's the thermal showing the people on board doing?" I asked.

"One in the pilothouse," Deuce said. "Four on the starboard rail, and three moving aft, probably on a lower deck. Their signature is fainter."

"Keep talking," I said to Deuce. "They'll do something."

"Two of the three are now stationary on the lower deck," he said after a moment. "The third is moving forward now. Still four on the rail and one in the pilothouse."

"It's the Minniches," Waldrup said. "They just locked them in an aft cabin."

"Which side are the two stationary ones?" I asked.

"Starboard, near the engine room, but not lost in the heat signature. The one that went aft with them has just joined the four on the rail. Still one in the pilothouse."

"You're sure they're on the lower deck?"

"Affirmative," Deuce said. "The third person appeared to climb a ladder to reach the others on the rail."

"We barely have enough fuel to get home at cruising speed," I said. "A few high-speed passes might get them to surrender, but that'll cost us a lot of gas."

"We can get more to you," Deuce said. "Binkowski's on his way back down here in a Feeb chopper. What's your idea?"

"Stop being an impatient buzzard," I replied and hit the throttles. The big racing boat roared ahead, and

I made a wide sweeping turn back toward the disabled boat. Even under the old rules of engagement, we were free to engage. We'd been fired on.

# CHAPTER TWENTY-SIX

The deckhands had been sitting around an up-turned box on the foredeck, playing cards and smoking cigarettes. Darius figured it'd been nearly an hour since they'd hoisted anchor and left the little cove. They were still in international waters, of that he was sure. He hadn't heard the other boat again.

"Can I ask you something?" Darius asked Ilya. He'd told them they were free to move about on the boat, if they liked. But Darius had chosen to stay in the pilot-house.

"You want to know how much money you will receive," Ilya said, grinning.

Darius nodded. "I can't help it. I'm a businessman now."

"A valid question, Mister Minnich. But, considering that you will also have your life, what monetary gain do you think will be a fair gain above that?"

Darius thought about it a moment, uncertain about putting an actual figure to it. "You said half."

"Yes, I did," Ilya replied. "However, I could say any number and reduce that to a third, and it will still be on top of your lives. I like to think I'm a fair business-man, like yourself. If this suit is everything it is reput-ed to be, my clients will pay dearly to make it impervi-ous to the Americans' attempts to shut it down. I plan to begin negotiations at five million American dollars and will probably settle on four million. My clients are fanat-ics. Very rich, but fanatics nonetheless. You will get half."

One corner of Darius's mouth rose almost imper-ceptibly. Looking through the windshield, Ilya didn't no-tice. But Celia noticed and it disheartened her. With two million dollars, she and Darius could live like royalty in quite a few places.

*But at what cost to our souls?* she thought.

Suddenly, gunfire erupted from the back of the boat. Darius recognized the roaring sound that followed and confirmed it when he looked back and saw a racing boat accelerating away to the west.

Darius stared as a man in the boat raised a small, sinister-looking gun and began firing at the fishing boat. Darius could have sworn there were several more men lying on the bow before it disappeared in the darkness.

Ilya shouted orders to the men on the foredeck and said something to Oleg, who'd been standing just inside the pilothouse door.

"Oleg will return you to your cabin," Ilya said. "Stay there and stay down, until I find out what is going on."

Oleg raised his weapon and motioned with it. Dari-us helped Celia down the short ladder to the dining area, then they retraced their steps to the cabin on the lower deck. Oleg once more locked them inside.

"What's going on?" Celia asked. "Was that gunfire?"

"Yes," Darius replied, listening intently. He could no longer hear the racing boat, and a screeching sound from the engine room just behind their cabin didn't bode well for Ilya being able to make a run for Cuban waters. There was a muffled boom and the engine went dead, leaving them in total silence for a moment.

"A racing boat attacked us," Darius said. "I heard it earlier, as we were just leaving the island. It was a long way off and slowed down."

"Do you think they know we're aboard?"

"I'm certain of it," he replied. "I got a glimpse of it, just after the shots were fired. It's one of those superfast racing boats, and I could swear it was Miguel that was shooting back."

"Miguel?" Celia gasped. "But how?"

"I don't know, but he's not alone out there. I saw at least four other men on that boat. His security team, maybe."

The sounds of men shouting directly above them cut the discussion short. Then the roar of the powerful boat's engines penetrated the hull. It seemed to be racing at high speed in a circle around the front of the fishing boat.

Seconds later, Darius heard Ilya shouting orders, obviously very angry. Heavy footsteps sounded above as the men ran forward, then crossed the work deck to the other rail.

Rifle and handgun fire could be heard from the other side of the boat, and seconds later the roar of the racing boat went by so close and at such a high rate of speed that Darius was certain the men on deck had little chance of hitting it.

As the speedboat passed, more gunshots erupted, this time sounding like several machine guns. Darius grabbed Celia and forced her to the deck. He then lay over top of her as he heard two loud splashes.

Anguished screams came from above, and the shooting ceased. From the sound of the engines, the racing boat had moved off quite a distance and slowed down, Miguel perhaps contemplating making another pass. Wails of men in pain and shouted orders followed. Above it all, Ilya yelled fanatically.

It became quiet for a few minutes, an occasional moan from above and a tinny voice on the radio all they heard. Another minute passed, then loud footsteps came running down the hallway.

Darius rose and helped his wife to her feet. "Are you okay?" he asked, very concerned.

"Yes," Celia replied. "Are you alright?"

Before Darius could answer, the door flew open. Oleg stepped inside, his gun pointed at Darius and Celia. He strode into the cabin and backhanded Celia, knocking her back onto the bunk.

Oleg put the barrel of the handgun to Darius's chest, pushing him back with it, and growled, "What did you do?"

# CHAPTER TWENTY-SEVEN

When we came out of the turn, I lined the Cigarette up with the port side of the *Esperanza*, pushing the throttles to the stops. The boat surged forward, both engines howling a throaty roar, as I aimed for a spot about twenty feet off the fishing boat's port side. Knowing we would probably take fire, I began a series of zigs and zags, the bow turning away from a spot twenty feet out from the fishing boat with each zig.

Seeing the muzzle flashes from the guns on the deck and hearing the occasional crack of a near miss, we bore down on the old boat. All four in back had moved to the port gunwale, MP-5s at the ready. This was going to be the modern version of a pirate's broadside fusillade.

I timed it perfectly, turning away from the boat just ten feet from it, and all five machine guns opened up at once, raking the port rail and pilothouse with hundreds of rounds in a matter of seconds. The ejected casings littered the deck of the Cigarette.

The spray from our wake and rooster tail washed over the rail of the *Esperanza*, and as I looked back, two men were swept overboard. I didn't know how many were hit, but they'd been clustered close together and none were still standing, so there was a good chance several were dead or injured. We'd passed very close, the team all aiming upward and away from the captives on the lower deck.

By this point we were convinced it was the Minniches. Deuce had pretty much confirmed it in our minds when we were making the wide turn. He'd said that Darlene Minnich had finally admitted to letting an Eastern European black market group know about the Minniches' travel plans.

Half a mile astern of the *Esperanza*, I brought the Cigarette down to an idle and killed the engines. Nodding at Jeremiah, I said, "Hey, Deuce, I think now would actually be a good time to give Germ's idea a try. I think that fishing boat is in distress."

I'd said it in jest, but it wasn't a bad idea. We were very close to Cuban waters, and the longer we sat out here, the more dangerous the situation became.

"Give it a try," Deuce said. "Hail them and tell them to heave to and stand by to be boarded."

So I did just that. I let ten seconds slowly tick by. Then I took the VHF mic in my hand again. "*Última Esperanza*, heave to and prepare to be boarded. We will not advise again."

The radio crackled and a man said, "If you try to take us, we will kill our hostages."

"*Esperanza*, we are going to board you," I repeated and started the engines. "Have everyone aboard standing on the starboard rail with their hands behind their heads."

Engaging the transmissions, I brought the Cigarette up to ten knots and slowly moved around to approach the disabled vessel with the moon at our backs.

"Jesse," Deuce said. "You only have about five minutes. Satellite radar shows a MiG-29 just took off from San Antonio de los Benos Airfield, one hundred and seventy miles from your location."

"A MiG? You gotta be shitting me."

"Be advised, Binkowski is inbound to you now. He has fuel and two of the boxes from the *Revenge*. Also, two F-15 Eagles are scrambling from Homestead. They're only slightly closer than the MiG."

*One of the boxes from the Revenge?* I thought. *The minigun? On a chopper against a MiG?* Hopefully, the Eagles would get here first.

A hundred yards from the other boat, I slowed. Most of the lights on the *Esperanza* were out. Idling forward, Scott and Jeremiah moved up to the second seat and the spot in between. Both men were exceptional shots with the short-barreled MP-5.

Only four people stood on the rail. As we drew nearer, I could see that one was a woman, wearing torn slacks and a shirt tied loosely in front.

"That's definitely Mister and Missus Minnich," Waldrup said, looking through the monocular.

"That's far enough!" one of the people on the rail shouted. "If you come any closer, we'll kill them!"

Dropping the throttles to neutral, I shut off the engines, letting the Cigarette continue forward of its own momentum. I reached down, took my own Tavor from my go bag, and brought it up. None of the people on the deck seemed to be wearing any kind of night vision.

The moon was nearing the western horizon and for the kidnappers, the Cigarette was silhouetted before it. Hopefully, they wouldn't notice the fact that we were drifting toward them.

"Is that all of your crew?" I shouted, bringing the Tavor up and aiming at the man nearest the bow. We could now clearly see that two men, one with a shaved head and the other with short, light-colored hair, held the Minniches between them. The Minniches both seemed to have their hands tied behind their backs and had handguns pointed at their heads.

The man standing next to Darius Minnich leaned a little away from him and shouted, "Our crew is all dead. These are hostages. If you try to come any closer, we will kill them."

"I have the guy on the right," I whispered as the Cigarette continued to slowly drift toward the *Esperanza*. "Scott, you take the guy on the left, when Germ counts down."

I didn't reply to the kidnapper, just let the momentum of the go-fast boat slowly carry us closer and closer. With the moon behind us, I counted on them not detecting that we were getting nearer as the seconds ticked by in silence.

"On one," Jeremiah said. "Three, two...."

The man to the left of Mister Minnich moved suddenly and shouted, "I said no closer."

"One," Jeremiah whispered. Time seemed to slow down then. Scott and I both fired at the same time, and Jeremiah fired just a fraction of a second later. As my

Tavor kicked, I knew without looking away from my target that Minnich was dead. A spraying mist partially blocked my view of the man in my sights.

At precisely the same time, the woman stomped on the bald guy's instep and threw her left shoulder up. The man's gun went off at the same instant that my bullet entered his head, just above his left eye.

I swung my sights to the left, but the other man was already falling backward. Darius Minnich crumpled where he stood, and his wife tumbled forward over the rail, screaming as she fell toward the water.

"Take the helm!" I shouted as I stripped off the night vision goggles and stepped out of my boat shoes. "Search the boat," I said to Andrew, climbing quickly over the windshield. "But be fast. We only have four minutes."

In four quick steps, I dove from the bow at a dead sprint, stretching as far as I could for the water. Celia Minnich hit the water when I was just going over the windshield, her scream ending abruptly as she went under.

Never taking my eyes from the spot where she submerged until the last second, I hit the water. Holding the knife position, I opened my eyes, for all the good it did. I was surrounded by inky blackness, no light at all to indicate up from down or allow me to judge distance.

Knowing without seeing, I figured she'd hit the water with her lungs empty from the scream. The impact would cause her to inhale sharply and her system would go into sudden shock, paralyzed by the water in her lungs.

I began kicking and stroking with my arms, swimming downward at an angle to where I calculated the best chance was to catch her before she sank into sixteen hundred feet of blackness, never to be seen again.

My lungs began to burn and the pressure on my ears was excruciating. Somewhere in my subconscious, I knew that if I didn't equalize the pressure soon, my eardrums would rupture, causing vertigo. Then I'd join Celia Minnich in the slow fall into the abyss.

When I felt like I couldn't go another stroke without taking a breath, I dug deep and went further, the pressure in my ears telling me I was at least twenty feet down and in serious trouble. Exhausted and out of oxygen, my lungs and shoulders burned, every fiber of my being telling me to go up.

Just as I started to turn and kick for the surface, my foot hit something soft and yielding. I quickly scissored my body and dove, knowing that I was surely about to drown. When I reached out my hands to stroke once more, my right hand tangled in something soft and wispy. I grabbed it and pulled. It was her hair. I pulled harder as I turned and began kicking toward the surface.

Celia Minnich's inert body came up with me, and I reached down, hooked an arm, and hauled her up into a better position. With my other hand, I clawed at the water, my legs kicking with abandon.

Deuce's dad, Russ, had once taught me some of the finer arts of free diving. He'd said that the body's urge to breathe was based more on its need to expel carbon dioxide than to take in oxygen. Somehow my subconscious mind took over and I calmed myself, slowly letting air bubble out of my nose as I swam upward toward a bright light.

I'd heard stories about near-death experiences and the bright light. What it was, I didn't know. Somewhere in my mind, I knew that if I could just get to the light, everything would be okay.

It seemed like a lifetime later that my head broke the surface, my lungs long empty. The cold rush of welcome air filled my lungs as I gasped and choked.

A roaring sound filled my ears as hands grabbed at me, taking Celia Minnich and pulling her up. More hands grabbed me and I was hauled out of the water, completely drained but now certain that I was going to live.

The roaring sound, as well as the bright light, seemed to be coming from above. I suddenly recognized it as a helicopter. Binkowski had arrived.

As I struggled to get to my feet, I began to hear voices again. Andrew's calm baritone voice said, "Okay, lower him down, Jeremy. Deuce, we have both victims on board and a laptop computer. The man's dead and beyond help. Administering CPR to the woman."

I stumbled as I tried to get to the helm and nearly fell overboard. "You okay, Gunny?" Scott asked, steadying me.

Waldrup was on all fours, doing CPR on Celia Minnich. Blood stained the left shoulder of her blouse. Looking back at where her husband's body had been lowered by Jeremy and Jeremiah, I knew there was no need for CPR on him. Apparently the bullet had entered just behind his right ear and exited in a fist-sized hole from his left temple.

I struggled to get over the first seat and dropped into it. "Is everyone on board?" I yelled.

"Yeah," Andrew replied. "Deuce says to get the fuck outta here."

The engines were already running, and I slipped them into gear and idled away from the *Esperanza*. "Somebody give me a spare earwig!" I shouted.

One was produced and I powered it on, adjusting it to my ear. Deuce was talking in a calm voice. "Eagles inbound, ten miles out. They'll get there first. Get out now. Head north."

I hit the throttles and the Cigarette jumped up onto plane. I had no night vision, but I could clearly make out the Big Dipper and turned the boat in the direction the pointer stars said to go.

In seconds we were moving away from the *Esperanza* at ninety knots as Deuce's voice came over the earwig. "Sink the boat as soon as they're clear."

Looking back for a second, I saw the *Esperanza* lit up by the spotlight on the black Bell helicopter, which hovered broadside to it about a hundred feet away. Suddenly a line of fire stitched the darkness, and even over the sound of the racing engines at full throttle, I heard the ripping noise of the minigun. Just as I looked back to the front, the sky behind us lit up bright orange, and a moment later, the shock wave and then the sound of the explosion overtook us.

"Holy shit," I heard Jeremy say.

I switched the VHF to the frequency monitored by the 125th Air Wing out of Homestead and snatched the mic. "Inbound Eagles, this is DHS vessel in distress."

"Hey, Homey," a voice came back over the speaker, with a decided Texas drawl. "Cowboy here, with Rat Tail on my wing. What can Snake do for you fellas this early in the morning?"

Grinning, I said, "I have a friendly rotary at my six, Cowboy, and an inbound tango not far behind him."

"Roger that, Homey," Cowboy said. "I got 'em both on tactical." Then in fluent Tex-Mex Spanish, he said, "This here's a pair of Florida Air National Guard F-15 Eagles calling the inbound MiG-29 approaching a civilian watercraft in international waters. If we're gonna dance, I'm leading, amigo."

Someone pushed a set of night vision goggles onto my head and I reached up to adjust the fit. Suddenly, two jets shrieked past, just barely above the water. In the gray-green of the night vision, they appeared as nothing more than a streak, leaving a wake of disturbed water behind them. I looked back and saw the two pairs of distinctive twin exhausts set close together. They suddenly glowed white hot as the jet jockeys kicked in the afterburners, and both planes climbed and turned westward, spreading out to engage the approaching MiG, if necessary.

"Looks like I'm not getting my dance card punched, Homey," Cowboy said. "My dance partner is bugging out."

The helicopter caught up to us and slowed, matching our speed. "Roger that, Cowboy," I said into the mic. "Appreciate the help. If you guys get up to Marathon, ask around for the *Anchor*. I'll buy you a beer."

Hearing a coughing sound, I looked down between the seats. Waldrup rose a little and helped Celia Minnich up to a sitting position as she continued to cough up seawater. Waldrup quickly tore his shirt off and wrapped it around the woman's shoulders.

"Welcome back, Missus Minnich," he said as she continued coughing. He looked up at me. "You got a first aid kit? A blanket or a towel?"

"Poncho liner in my bag," I said. "There's QuickClot and bandages in there, too."

Digging through my go bag, he pulled the Quick Clot out and pulled Missus Minnich's blouse down over her shoulder. The bullet had passed through the fleshy part of her shoulder, back to front, leaving a nasty exit wound. As Waldrup poured most of the powder onto the wound, her head went back, brows furrowed in pain. She barely made a sound as Waldrup slapped a bandage on the wound. Then he did the same with the entry wound on the back of her shoulder.

Satisfied, Waldrup took my poncho liner from my go bag and wrapped it around the woman's shoulders over his shirt. He then helped her get into the second seat and strapped her in. His chest bare, Waldrup knelt and shielded her view into the rear cockpit, where her husband lay dead on the deck.

"Hey," I heard Binkowski's voice over the VHF. "You guys looking for a gas station?"

"About eight miles dead ahead," I said into the mic. "South Anguilla Cay, the first island you'll see. On the west side, you should find a Zodiac beached near the north end. Drop the tanks in the water near there."

The nose of the chopper dropped and the sound of the blades changed pitch as it began to move ahead of us. Minutes later, I slowed as I entered the cove, but didn't drop off plane. We quickly located the gas cans and began pouring the precious fuel into the nearly empty tanks, while Andrew and Jeremy waded to the spot where they'd beached the Zodiac.

In minutes, they dragged the inflatable out to where we floated and pulled the motor, handing it and the gas tank up to Waldrup, who muscled the heavy engine into the forward cabin. While Andrew and Jeremy deflated the boat, Scott and I poured the last gas can into the tank. Andrew lifted the partially folded and rolled-up boat to Waldrup, and he stashed it forward also.

Celia Minnich was awake and breathing normally, watching as the men climbed back aboard before looking up at me. "You're not with Miguel's security team."

"No, ma'am," I replied quietly.

"Darius?"

I looked into her eyes. With all that she'd been through, and I could only imagine what that was, she still had a steely toughness in her blue eyes.

"I'm sorry, ma'am," I said. "Your husband didn't make it."

The news didn't seem to have any effect. Most women would have begun sobbing, yelling, or something. She just stared back at me with quiet acceptance. "Miguel said it was you that dove in and saved me."

"Yes, ma'am."

As Waldrup knelt down next to her, and I restarted the engines, she mouthed, "Thank you."

I only nodded as I slowly backed the boat away from shore and turned northeast toward the gap between here and Bellows Cay to the north.

"Hey, Homey," a voice on the radio said. "You still there?"

"Heading north," I replied.

"The CO just contacted me in person," Cowboy said, obviously impressed. "I don't know who you guys are, but we've been ordered to remain on station with y'all until you get back to wherever you're going."

"Tell the colonel he's welcome at the *Anchor,* too," I said and shoved the throttles to the stops, turning through the gap and heading north for Dog Rocks and the turn home.

# EPILOGUE

**M**ore details came to light over the following days. Darlene Minnich claimed she'd only wanted to hurt her ex-husband's business when she'd told the kidnappers about the project he was working on and his travel plans. She'd sworn that they'd agreed to only hold him until he gave up the technology of his company's CephaloSuit. She'd been arrested and charged with conspiracy to commit murder and kidnapping.

◆ ◆ ◆ ◆

Parsons came down to my island the day after we returned and brought CephaloTech's COO, Delores Juarez, to extend her thanks for the rescue mission. "Missus Minnich is recovering in the hospital, or she would have come herself," Delores said.

"I'm sorry we weren't able to save Mister Minnich," I said, uncomfortable with the situation. "What's the future of the company look like without him?"

"Business as usual, Mister McDermitt. Another reason I asked Dave to bring me here. We'll be exhibiting the new suit in a week, and based on Dave's description of your background, Missus Minnich asked me to extend an invitation to you for the unveiling. You'll find the surroundings familiar. It will be at Camp Lejeune. The project leader is anxious to meet you."

I hesitantly agreed. I like my life here and don't like to leave. But the idea of seeing just what this technology might mean to my brothers in Force Recon definitely had an appeal, so I accepted. Though I couldn't be certain, there seemed to be some chemistry going on between Parsons and Delores Juarez.

Marty wasn't on hand during the takedown, but that didn't stop Deuce from giving him full credit for organizing the assets to solve the kidnapping and rescue Missus Minnich so quickly. He received a personal commendation from the sheriff, which came directly from Travis's desk at the Pentagon. Travis had said he would like to be there, but had to fly to Bogotá. After the ceremony, Marty was given three days' leave and chose to go up and spend it with Kim in Gainesville.

The following Friday, Linda and I were at the *Anchor* catching up with Rusty and readying the *Island Hopper*

for the flight to North Carolina. Pescador lifted his head from where he was lying beside me and looked toward the driveway. A blue sedan pulled into the parking lot.

Rusty nodded toward it and said, "Who the hell you reckon that might be?"

I looked out the window as the passenger door and both back doors opened. The car had a blue tag with a colonel's insignia on the bumper. I grinned as a tall young man in a cowboy hat held the door to the bar open for another young man and an older man with salt-and-pepper hair.

The older man stood just inside the door as his eyes adjusted to the dim interior. Finally, he strode toward the bar and addressed Rusty. "I was told we might find a friend here."

"A bit early for that beer, Cowboy," I said to the tall Texan.

He turned to where Linda and I sat at the end of the bar, drinking our coffee.

"Glad to see you're alright, Homey."

I approached him and extended my hand. "Jesse McDermitt."

Taking my hand and glancing quickly at Linda, then back to me, he removed his hat and nodded. "Neil Thornton," he said. "This is Terence 'Rat Tail' Lowe and Colonel Joseph 'Quickdraw' Quick."

"Just call me Joe, Jesse," the colonel said, extending his hand. "I haven't been behind a stick in a decade."

Rusty poured coffee for the three pilots and they sat down.

"Mister McDermitt is the one that invited us, Colonel," Cowboy said.

"The call I got that night," Joe said after taking a sip of his coffee. "Hey, this is good."

"Rusty gets it from a little farm in Costa Rica called La Minita."

Joe raised his mug and nodded to Rusty, then continued. "Anyway, the call I got that night. It came from the top."

"Secretary of the Air Force?" I asked.

"No," Joe said. "That's what got me curious, so I decided to take you up on the offer you made to Major Thornton, here. The call I got was from the secretary's boss."

"Oh," Rusty said, jerking a thumb toward a framed photograph over the bar. "You mean this guy here? He went fishing with Jesse once." It was a picture of President George Bush in the Oval Office with me, Rusty, and his daughter, Julie, standing around him.

Looking at the picture, Joe smiled. "Yeah, that'd be the guy." He chuckled and looked at me. "Don't suppose you can share anything about what you and your *fishing party* were doing so close to Cuban waters?"

"Sorry, Colonel," I replied with a wink. "I'm just a guy who likes to fish."

We talked for a little longer, and Joe said he'd contact my charter office by email to arrange a charter. Though Kim is several hundred miles away, she likes to take care of my website and charters. So, wherever her laptop is, that's where my charter office is located.

"I hate to cut this short," I said, nodding out the window to where the *Hopper* sat at the top of the boat ramp. "But Linda and I were about to take off for North Carolina to spend the weekend."

Joe glanced out the window and his eyes grew wide. "Is that a Beaver? You ever charter in it?"

"Yeah," I replied, picking up my flight bag from the deck. "It's a Beaver. I can take you up to some of the best bass spots in the Everglades, or redfish off Cape Sable."

The three of them followed me and Linda out to the ramp. They enviously inspected the *Hopper*, while we loaded and secured our bags in the back.

"I'd like to take you up on that," Joe said, turning toward me. "Bass fishing from a Beaver sounds like great fun. I used to fly one in Alaska."

I handed him a business card with my name and Kim's website on it as I climbed in. "Rates are on the website, Colonel. I'll even let you fly her."

The men backed away when I started the big radial engine and eased the *Hopper* into the water.

The following morning, a car picked me and Linda up at our hotel in Jacksonville, North Carolina. Half an hour later, we pulled into the parking lot at the rifle range on Camp Lejeune. The driver stayed with the car, Pescador sleeping in the front passenger seat.

Celia Minnich was waiting for us as we walked up to crowd of people assembled at the top of the firing range. She was accompanied by Delores Juarez, Dave Parsons, and Miguel Waldrup. Surprisingly, Meg Stewart was with the big security man.

"I'm so glad you came," Missus Minnich said, her left arm still in a sling.

"Well, from what Parsons told me, I was curious." I looked around. Bleachers had been set up behind and to either side of the range coach's tower at the five-hundred-yard line. A lot of high-ranking officers and enlisted sat in most of the stands, along with some influential people in business suits. All of them were looking downrange, as if waiting for something to happen.

"I would have thought y'all would use the infiltration course out at Force Recon," I said.

"For other kinds of equipment, perhaps," Celia said. "Our suit is designed to be used in open terrain."

"Well, it doesn't get more open than this," I said, looking downrange at the butts. "When does the exhibit begin?"

Looking at his watch, Waldrup said, "It started thirty-three minutes ago. Come and have a seat. We have a spot on the front row just for you, Gunny."

Shrugging, I followed them to the bleachers, where we all sat down in front of the top brass of the armed forces. Celia left us there and walked to the podium.

"My apologies for the interruption," she said, arranging a notepad in front of her. "Some of you may know our special guest, retired Marine Gunnery Sergeant Jesse McDermitt."

I heard a few *oohrah* grunts from behind me and a smattering of applause. Celia continued her speech.

"I trust that during the delay, all of you had a chance to scour the field ahead. Major Roberts has been making his way toward us for the last thirty-five minutes and will be making his location known in just a few more minutes."

She stopped talking and turned to look out over the range. I followed her gaze. Parsons had said it was some kind of high-tech ghillie suit that made the wearer invisible. I studied the terrain, my eyes moving across the grassy area between the five-hundred and three-hundred-yard lines. If the man in the suit was about to reveal his location, I figured he'd be in this area.

There was nothing there but grass. A light wind was blowing from left to right, occasionally flattening the grass, which looked like it should have been mowed before an exhibit like this.

Celia turned back toward the podium, holding a hand to her ear. Glancing at me, she said, "Ladies and gentlemen, my tech people have just informed me that Major Roberts has reached his target. I present to you, Major Frank Roberts, United States Marine Corps, wearing the next generation in infiltration technology, the McDermitt Suit."

I looked at Celia in surprise, and suddenly the grass in front of me flickered and turned silver. Less than ten feet away, directly in front of me, the silver blanket rose and a man's face and body appeared. He was grinning from ear to ear. Probably because my mouth was hanging open.

Extending his hand and stepping toward me, he said, "It's an honor to finally meet you, Gunny."

You could have knocked me over with a feather. All around, the spectators applauded and some of the higher-ranking generals and admirals rose and went to the podium, all of them asking Celia questions at one time.

Standing up slowly, I couldn't help but grin as I took the major's hand. "It was Missus Minnich's idea," he said. "It's a fitting name for the latest in sniper technology."

The usual pomp and ceremony began, the band playing a motivational tune in the background as caterers quickly covered a table with finger foods and drinks. Most of the attendees crowded around Celia, until Waldrup inserted himself in front of her. The questions became more orderly then as he stood beside her, Meg dwarfed at his side.

Several minutes later, I got Parsons, Celia, and Waldrup off to the side. "I'm honored," I told her. "Your husband's technology is going to save a lot of lives."

"I believe it will," she said.

Looking at the bigger man, I asked, "Have you told her?"

Celia looked from me to Waldrup and back again, "Told me what?"

"No," Miguel said, "I figured that should come from you if it came from anyone."

I turned toward the car we'd arrived in and whistled loudly. The driver opened the front door, and Pescador stepped out of the car and stretched. For the last ten days, since we'd returned to the *Anchor* after bringing the yacht in, Pescador had been in a real funk. Listless and lazy, he had barely eaten in days. Seeing me, he trotted toward us, oblivious to the crowd of people behind us, trusting that if I was okay with it, he was, too.

Suddenly, the big dog stopped a few feet away and his eyes fell on Celia. She gasped, her good hand going to her mouth as her eyes filled. "Nadador?"

The big dog literally melted down right there on the spot, trotting to her and rolling on the ground at her feet, whimpering.

"How? What?" Celia stammered.

Though I hated even thinking about it, this was the right thing to do and had been the only thing on my mind for days.

"I found him up in the back country north of Big Pine Key, a day after Hurricane Wilma. I've been calling him Pescador."

Celia fell to her knees as Pescador writhed and rolled. She scratched his belly for a moment, then he stood up, his heavy rudder-like tail wagging his whole body.

"I thought he'd drowned," Celia said, looking up and sobbing.

Linda and I waited around for a few more minutes, then we said our goodbyes and started toward the car. My heart was torn. Pescador and I had become more than friends.

"It's the right thing to do," Linda said, taking my hand and leaning her head on my shoulder.

I heard him bark and turned around. He came trotting toward me, his tail almost taking him off his feet. When he got to us, he sat down in front of me and barked once.

"No, buddy," I said, my voice catching a little. "You need to stay here and take care of Celia."

As if he could understand what I was saying, he looked back to where she stood with the others. When he looked back, I knew that he understood.

Kneeling, I gave him a farewell scratch behind both ears and said, "Go on, boy. You're home now."

# THE END

If you'd like to receive my twice a month newsletter for specials, book recommendations, and updates on coming books, please sign up on my website:

WWW.WAYNESTINNETT.COM

THE CHARITY STYLES CARIBBEAN THRILLER SERIES
*Merciless Charity*
*Ruthless Charity* (Summer, 2016)
*Heartless Charity* (Winter, 2017)

THE JESSE MCDERMITT
CARIBBEAN ADVENTURE SERIES

*Fallen Out*
*Fallen Palm*
*Fallen Hunter*
*Fallen Pride*
*Fallen Mangrove*
*Fallen King*
*Fallen Honor*
*Fallen Tide*
*Fallen Angel*
*Fallen Hero* (Fall, 2016)

The Gaspar's Revenge Ship's Store is now open. There you can purchase all kinds of swag related to my books.
WWW.GASPARS-REVENGE.COM

# AFTERWORD

I t's very humbling for me to release this eighth novel in the Jesse McDermitt series. Jesse was a product of my imagination in the 1980s and the lead character in several short stories I wrote at the time. I never dreamed this character and this series would become so widely accepted and I'd be able to make a living telling Jesse's stories. It's been an enormously fun ride thus far, and I'm looking forward to many more adventures with Jesse.

I'd dreamed most of my life about being a writer. I know the stories in my mind are pretty good, but putting the words in just the right order was a learning experience, and I'm still learning. My dad was a hardworking man who had little formal education, yet he became a prominent builder in Central Florida. He once told me that he surrounded himself with brilliant people and simply directed what he wanted done and they made him look good.

So, I do the same. The story you just read didn't look like this when I finished writing it. My team of beta readers, editors, proofreaders, cover designers, and formatters are the best that I can find in their fields. They make the book look like the story in my head, just as Dad's team made his construction projects look like the plans in his head.

Made in United States
North Haven, CT
21 May 2024

52743641R00148